In The Slot

Chris Walters

Also by
Chris Walters

The Tashaverse:
No One Like You
Make It Real
Send Me An Angel

Goddess Good

Book Cover by Jaycee DeLorenzo

ISBN: 978-1-964292-10-6

eBook ISBN: 978-1-964292-11-3

Visit the link below to listen to the In The Slot playlist.

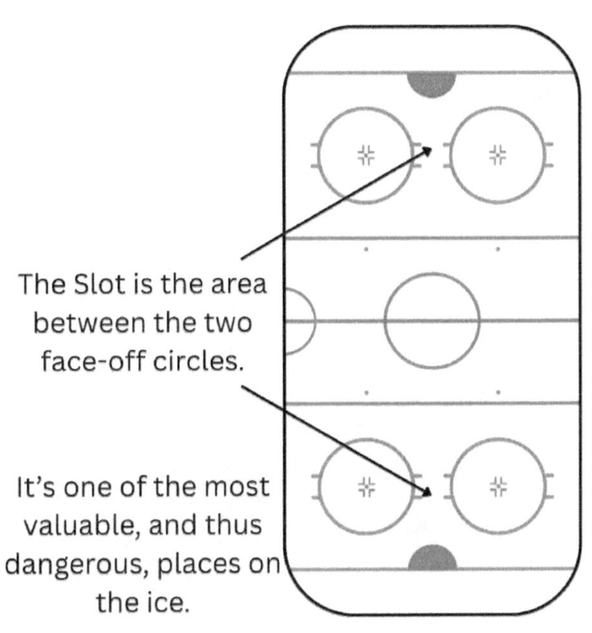

The Slot is the area between the two face-off circles.

It's one of the most valuable, and thus dangerous, places on the ice.

For everyone brave enough to follow their dreams.

For everyone willing to step beyond anything they've ever considered before and discover something new and amazing about themselves.

Content Awareness

- One of the MCs experiences extremely poor parenting (including homophobia).

- Sports violence

- Explicit sex between consenting adults

- Brief depictions of sex work **Author Note:** Sex work is work provided all involved are consenting adults. Human trafficking is immoral. I realize that in between these two statements are a vast amount of potentially morally gray areas of debate which many people may have strong feelings about. Furthermore, I recognize that we live in a world where many people – particularly in marginalized groups – are often driven into sex work by economic and social forces. Here in the United States in particular, we have a lot of work as a society that we can and should do to end trafficking, homelessness, food insecurity, persecution of LGBTQ+ individuals, and other significant drivers of nonconsensual sex work.

Contents

Chapter 1

Shoot You In The Back
Motörhead

Twelve years ago

The puck sailed down the ice on its way toward the empty net. A defender raced frantically after the speeding rubber disc in a valiant yet vain attempt to catch it, but everyone in the arena knew she wouldn't get there in time. The goal would be Keisha Owens' sixth, a double hat trick to seal a miraculous six to four victory in the state championship.

She never saw her final shot cross the goal line. As the puck rocketed inexorably toward the net, an unseen force struck a heavy blow to Keisha's back and catapulted her into the boards, crushing her in her moment of triumph. Pain erupted throughout Keisha's body, and she felt something snap in her legs. The last thing Keisha saw before she passed out was Olivia Kennedy's snarling face above her.

Keisha woke up in a strange room. She tried to process where she was, but everything felt foggy. There was an indescribable ache somewhere in her lower body, but her mind struggled to understand why. Something touched her hand and drew her eyes to the side. A person...someone...Mama...

The veil around Keisha's mind parted a bit more as one of Tamika Owens' hands touched her face. The other hand was wrapped firmly around her own. Keisha could see the muscles in her mother's hand straining, but she couldn't register the pressure. Another woman, dressed in blue, reached out and tapped her mother's hand. Keisha saw the muscles in Mama's hand relax, but still felt no pressure there.

"W..." Keisha coughed. Her throat wasn't working. It felt like someone had shoved a cotton ball in her esophagus. A cotton ball laced with poison ivy. The woman in blue placed a calming hand on her mother's shoulder before lifting a cup with a straw to Keisha's lips. She drank greedily, slightly soothing the irritation in her mouth and throat.

"What...happened?" Keisha croaked.

"You won the game, baby. You did it." Her mom had tears in her eyes.

"Mama, what's wrong? Why am I here?"

"Someone hit you, baby. You were injured badly."

Memory rushed in, and Keisha's skin crawled. She remembered the sickening sound as something broke. Her mind relived the nearly overwhelming rush of agony as bones snapped. Finally, her mind's eye gazed upon the cruel visage of the bitch who was responsible. Keisha knew she was in a hospital bed, and Olivia Kennedy was the reason.

A doctor came in. She flipped through the chart, her face a schooled mask of neutrality. "Ms. Owens. I'm Doctor Stafford. You've experienced a serious injury..."

Keisha tried to listen, to pay attention, to make sure she understood what the doctor was saying, but her mind rebelled. Out of the fog of words, she caught key phrases. Phrases such as: "...multiple fractures..." or "...chance to walk..." or worst of all, "...likely never skate again."

I've never done anything to Olivia Kennedy except finally beat her at her own game. Her jealousy was her problem before, and my revenge will be her penalty. I don't care if it takes me the rest of my life to get her back.

When the tears dried, reality set in. "Mama, how can we pay for this? What about your job?"

"Shh, it's okay, baby," her mother replied. "Someone set up a GoFundMe for us. We're gonna be okay. We'll get you the help you need. I promise."

"The doctor was talking, but I couldn't hear what she said. How bad is it?"

"It's bad, angel. But it's not so bad we can't get through it."

"Can I play again?"

Keisha saw the expression on her mother's face, and she knew the answer.

Lying in bed a few days later, Keisha listened to the beeping of the machines around her as her mind drifted back to her first meeting with Olivia Kennedy, almost ten years ago. Keisha was skating on a boys team back then, practicing for a metro area youth tournament. Her team wore hand-me-down gear which was often ill-fitting, but it was what they could afford. She recalled looking on with a hefty dose of jealousy when the Puck Princess and her team took the other end of the ice. Daughter of a professional hockey player and an Olympic speed skater, Olivia Kennedy was destined for the ice. According to rumors in the youth hockey world, she received private hockey lessons from the best tutors starting at age three.

She recalled the sneer when Olivia slid to a stop in a flurry of ice shavings. "What are you people doing in our rink?"

Her captain, Isaac, was quick to respond. "Practicing. What's it look like?"

"*Oh.* That's what you call it," Olivia sniffed. "Why don't we play for the ice? Twenty minutes, and the winner keeps practicing. If we tie, we share."

Keisha recalled the smirk on Isaac's face as he looked at the all-girl team behind the Puck Princess. "Deal." Isaac just saw girls, but Keisha observed well cared for, top-line gear. She knew her team was in trouble.

Twenty minutes later, her team skated off the ice, totally humiliated, the jeers of Olivia and her team filling their ears. Keisha's team lost every game in that tournament.

Keisha picked at her IV tube, trying to shut out the noise of the hospital beyond. She'd been in this bed for almost a month before she was cleared to leave, and now she wanted more than anything to be long gone. Even though Keisha wanted to go home, she also dreaded leaving the hospital in a wheelchair. Home would remind her of what she lost.

She reached out to squeeze her mother's hand. "Thank you, Mom."

"What for, baby?"

"For making me study as hard as I practice. I can still get a college degree, even if I can't skate. One more year of high school before college, though."

Tamika smiled down at her daughter. "Baby, you can do anything you set your mind to."

Keisha grimaced. She had a list of things on her mind. The top item on her list was walking again. Item number two was relearning how to skate. The third item was perhaps her favorite—find a way to exact revenge on Olivia Kennedy.

Her hopes for immediate justice were dashed when the state board announced a measly three-game suspension for Olivia the next season. Apparently, having immensely wealthy parents who are also state heroes meant getting away with no real consequences.

Keisha spent her summer leading into her senior year learning how to walk again. She attended every hockey practice, acting as the assistant coach. If Keisha couldn't skate, she'd do everything she could to help her high school team succeed from the bench.

Chapter 2

Burn In Hell
Twisted Sister

The flight into PDX had some of the best views in the country when the weather was clear, which it sometimes was in August. Of course, Olivia Kennedy would have had to look out her window to see those views. She hated Portland, even though she'd never been here before. Portland was a symbol of the long string of failures in her life. Three years of playing professional hockey in New York, and now she was playing on the other side of the country for an expansion team in a city no one expected to even get a team. Worse, she'd been traded by New York as a means to protect themselves in the expansion draft. A two-time Olympian reduced to trade bait. Sure, she'd had a few off years lately, but she was Olivia Kennedy, the Puck Princess.

I remember how I hated that nickname when I first heard it. My parents didn't understand, but Andrej got it. Of course it was my hockey tutor who took better care of me than my own parents. He said, "Olivia, if you let this name bother you, then you give your enemies power over you. Instead, you must embrace being the Puck Princess. Then you hold the power, not them." Andrej was right.

Thinking of holding the power, this is my year to turn things around. I'm going to kill it in Portland and play my way back into a trade to a real hockey city like Boston, Minneapolis, Montréal, or even Toronto. Once I am back to my old self, any of these teams would be lucky to have me. With my skills and experience, I'm confident I can carry even luckless Toronto to a championship. I just needed to get my mojo back.

Her mojo included getting married to Maxim Kovalev. Olivia was well aware of the gorgeous Russian's complete inability to keep his dick in his pants. His reputation for running through puck bunnies was legendary. Her parents assured her he would change his ways once they were married, just like her father had, long ago. Olivia honestly didn't care, she just wanted the dumb blond to learn how to be discreet. Her fiancé was an incredibly gifted scorer on the ice, but his scoring ability in the bedroom lacked any panache. He was handsome, stupid, and wealthy, which was good enough for Olivia's parents, and she wanted to please her parents.

Looking around PDX on her way to baggage claim, she admitted that the quaint airport was nicer than JFK—although improving on JFK was not a high bar to clear. Olivia hauled her bags to the light rail, seething at the humiliation of using public transit. Her parents cut her off financially a few years ago when her points production declined. An "incentive," they called it, although she suspected their own financial challenges played a role. At least in New York, she lived in Maxim's condo. It was part of their unspoken agreement—she shared his fancy apartment, drove his luxury cars, and wore the fashionable clothes he bought for her, and she turned a blind eye to the many nights he spent in his *other* condo. Olivia felt the acid in her stomach churn, knowing he'd likely be boring a string of puck bunnies to tears with his unimaginative thrusting in *their* bed. She didn't miss the sex with Maxim at all—she worried about her engagement ending if their forced separation caused him to rethink their deal, and he replaced her with a younger model.

The sorry state of her finances only added to her anxiety. Her credit cards were already nearly maxed out, and now she had to worry about rent, food, and fashionable clothes. A lifetime of priv-ilege and reckless spending left her little aptitude or patience for budgeting.

Olivia ate take-out Chinese for dinner before sending Maxim some tasteful nudes to remind him she was still his fiancée. She made sure not to show any of her cheap apartment in the shots. Image was everything to Maxim, and he hated anything he considered low class. Olivia texted her agent, urging her to find some more lucrative modeling gigs.

I'm not sure which I need more right now: the money or the boost to my image and media presence. Probably, the money, but not by much. There are no cameras in this pissant town. Not like New York, where

Maxim and I were plastered all over the society pages and socials every time we stepped out. Shit. Maybe I do need the image boost more.

The next morning, Olivia stood outside the aging facility where she would be skating, willing herself to go in. Decades past its prime, about the best thing anyone could say about the coliseum is the ice was kept cold. Entering her new hockey home, Olivia shivered knowing she was in hockey Siberia. She was greeted by a giant pink, red, and white banner welcoming the Blossoms to their new home.

Of course the stupid name is rose-related, like so many things in the so-called Rose City. Unfortunately, the city already had the Thorns soccer team, leaving the hockey team with few options for a tough-sounding name. Volcanoes was another terrible choice, but at least it sounded powerful. Instead, fan voting settled on the Blossoms. What a putrid, simpering, and weak name. Ugh. And the colors. The red is fine. White, too. The Canadians make red and white pop on their uniforms. But pink...*why did they choose fucking pink? I swear the fans either hate us or this city just sucks.*

She stuffed her thoughts down and faked a smile when a staff person opened the door and ushered her inside. Players, coaches, and team staff members mingled in the lobby. The team's general manager, Miles Caine, stepped into the center of the crowd and called for attention. "Good morning, everyone. Welcome to the Rose City, Blossoms. We are very excited to have everyone here for our inaugural season. Expectations are always low for expansion teams, but we are confident this team will achieve greatness, even in the first year." Caine droned on, and Olivia quickly lost interest in his incessant blathering.

Olivia studied the team around her. The coach, Shelby Hicks, was a two-time Olympian with a strong track record as an assistant coach. This was her first head coaching gig, but expectations were high.

The towering brunette was Svetlana Kravchenko. Selected the back-up goalie for the Russian national team at age eighteen, Svetlana was *persona non grata* in her erstwhile homeland due to her vocal opposition to the current regime. She hadn't set foot in Russia in years out of fear of being arrested or worse.

Svetlana was speaking with Heike Schmidt and Daniella Cruz. Olivia was familiar with both after playing against them the past few years. The two defenders were opposites in many ways. Heike was nearly as tall as the goalie, cool-headed, with a wicked slap shot, and a reputation for leveling anyone unwary enough to lower their head in center ice. Daniella was below average height, lightning fast, and led the league in power play goals by a defender last year. Those two were likely to be valuable assets for the team on the blue line.

Misty Thomas was not far away, speaking with Karla Jensen. The pair played together for four years at the University of Minnesota, and Portland traded up in the draft to keep them together. Olivia eyed Misty warily, as she was the most likely competition for the topline center spot. Karla was a big power forward who took up space in front of the crease.

"Hi. I'm so excited you're here." Olivia's reverie was broken by a bubbly voice at her side. Looking over and slightly down, she met the eager gaze of a young woman with vibrant pink hair. "I'm Cathy Miller. So nice to meet you."

"Uh. Yeah. Same." Olivia tried and failed to place her face. "I'm sorry. You are?"

Cathy's disappointment was palpable, but brief. "I'm a rookie. I played four years at RIT."

"Welcome?" Olivia had no idea what to say.

"I'm so excited to play with you. I hope the coach puts us on the same line."

I don't. The last thing I need is to be saddled with mentoring an undrafted rookie free agent. She'll be lucky to make the team, although this is an expansion team, so who knows.

Olivia's lips curled up in a smile she hoped appeared genuine. "Coach will do what she thinks is best."

A hand clapped Olivia on the back. "Yes, she will." The hand was attached to the arm of Sophie LeBeau. At thirty-nine, the legendary five-time Olympian was at the tail end of her career. Olivia couldn't imagine Sophie was happy to finish out her journey in a backwater like Portland.

Caine finally wound down his speech to polite applause. Coach Hicks stepped up. "Thank you, Miles. I expect everyone to work hard and leave everything out on the ice. We have less than three months until the season starts, so there's plenty to do. One other thing, do *not* embarrass the team off the ice. Spend the next hour and change getting your shit together. Practice starts at one o'clock sharp."

The locker room was absolute chaos. Portland's men's hockey team commanded the hockey locker room in the building, so the Blossoms were shoehorned into the old basketball team locker room, with two skaters sharing each cubby. When not in this building, they'd be sharing the men's team's practice facility most of the time, but Coach wanted them to get the feel of their new home. To Olivia's disgust, she had to share her cubby with Cathy Miller. The girl was a chatterbox who kept up an endless stream of gushing comments in Olivia's ear.

As soon as she was geared up, Olivia made her way out onto the ice to start stretching. There was something pure about fresh ice which soothed her soul. The familiar chill felt perfect as she got down on the ice to start her routine. Olivia always stretched the identical way, using the same techniques she had learned when she first took the ice almost thirty years ago. She wished she still loved the game like she did so long ago, too.

Over the years, Olivia learned to ignore the taunts about being a dirty player. She found it more difficult to ignore the constant whispers about how she lifted the championship cup her senior year only because Keisha Owens still wasn't able to walk. The insinuation of her inferiority nagged at her constantly.

Then there were the murmurings implying the U.S. could have won gold multiple times, if only Olivia hadn't destroyed the career of a generational talent. Each time she missed a pass at a world championship or whiffed on a shot in the Olympics, she felt the weight of the responsibility of Keisha Owens' absence from the American squad.

Finally, there were the internet chat rooms and message boards where keyboard warriors painted her as a thuggish brute. Badly edited photos of her wielding a hockey stick like an axe or sword were childishly amusing, but there was far worse out there. At first, it was bigoted commentators lurking in the darkest corners of the internet, but in recent years, there were growing numbers of people who felt emboldened to openly praise her for keeping hockey "pure" by eliminating a Black skater. Knowing people thought this about her made her physically ill.

As much as the smell and feel of fresh ice soothes me, the carved and chipped ice of every practice and game slowly gnaws at my will to continue playing. I know I am a husk of the player I had been as a teenager—or could still be. I've been going through the motions like an automaton for years. I need to turn my life around, but I'm not even sure if I care enough anymore. I chose to wear the number ninety-eight when I was a kid—a symbol of my desire to be spoken of next to Gretzky. Every time I put on my jersey the number mocks me now.

Chapter 3

Stronger

Britney Spears

Keisha stepped onto the ice for practice, her first steps habitually cautious. Each and every time she strapped on her skates, she recalled how it took until her senior year of college before she was cleared to skate again. The doctors called her a marvel. Her mother called it a miracle. Keisha called it returning home. She spent her first three years of college as an assistant to the coaching staff. As a student, she wasn't allowed to coach, but her coaches gave her substantial leeway to aid in training, development, and strategy. During her medical exile from playing the sport, she developed a deeper view of the game and the players. Resuming skating her senior year didn't change anything except letting her assist the other student athletes on the ice. Getting back on skates was a victory, but even then she was still years away from contact.

Securing her stick behind the bench, Keisha skated laps to loosen up her legs and mind. Even after three years of rec league hockey, followed by three more years of semi-pro, the old anxieties were still there. *Will my body hold up? Will I get injured again?*

She waved up into the stands at her friend Sharon. Sharon's oldest kid, Liza, was interested in playing hockey, so sometimes Sharon brought her to watch Keisha skate. She smiled at Liza, putting on a brave face, before beginning her stretches. Chuck Rhodes, the team's coach and captain, skated up to Keisha, asking for advice on strategy against their next opponent. Keisha talked Chuck into some line changes to better match up against the Bobcats' strengths and exploit their weaknesses.

Chuck's a good guy and an effortless leader, but he's definitely had his bell rung a few too many times. Stubborn as a goat whenever anyone suggests he hang up his skates. He's pushing fifty, though. I'm gonna miss him when he does finally call it a career.

After practice, Keisha hugged Sharon and Liza before meeting the rest of her Vipers teammates at the sports bar around the corner. She nursed her lager while she talked about holiday plans with the guys on her team and idly watched the screens. Keisha was viewing the Bruins-Rangers game when her phone rang. She didn't recognize the number or 503 area code, so she ignored it. Her phone buzzed again. And again.

Her goalie, Rick, asked, "You gonna get your phone?"

"Nah. Don't know the number."

"They keep calling. Might be important."

Her phone rang a fourth time, and she gave it a grumpy look. "Fine. I'll take it. If it's a telemarketer, then I'm passing it to you." She answered, "Hello?"

A tenor voice queried, "Hi, is this Keisha Owens?"

Keisha's voice was wary. "Yeah. Who's asking?"

"My name is Miles Caine. I'm the general manager of the Portland Blossoms. We'd like to sign you to a ten-day contract with the possibility of a full contract to follow."

"Not a fucking chance," Keisha hissed before she hung up.

Chuck saw her slam her phone down on the table. "Damn, who got you so pissed off?"

Keisha tried to play it off as nothing. "No one special. Just the general manager of the Portland Blossoms offering me a ten-day contract."

"You said yes, right?"

"*Hell no.* I told him to fuck off."

Chuck snickered. "He didn't listen cuz your phone's ringing again."

"I know damn well it's ringing," Keisha growled.

"Keisha, it's a *professional* contract. You can go pro. This is a huge opportunity for you." By now, the rest of the team was following along, nodding their support.

"You don't understand. Any other team, I would at least consider it—maybe even jump at the chance, but not the fucking Blossoms."

Her phone rang a sixth time, and she answered it this time. "*What part of* fuck off *didn't you understand?*" She screamed into the phone before she slammed it down again.

Chuck frowned, his expression deeply concerned. Keisha knew she never went off like this in front of the team. "Come on, let's talk," he commanded, using his captain's voice. They grabbed their coats and shuffled into the frigid Minneapolis air. "What's going on, Keisha?"

"You know about my injury. Well, the bitch who blindsided me plays for the Blossoms."

He nodded. "Yeah, I'm very well aware of where Olivia Kennedy plays."

Keisha winced at Chuck's mention of *her* name. "Are you? She ruined *my life.* The doctors said I'd never skate again. Hell, there was a chance I would never walk again."

"And yet here you are, walking and skating. You're good, Keisha. No, good doesn't cut it. You are incredible. If we had any passing ability on our team, you would be scoring five goals a game. The Blossoms are offering you a dream opportunity."

"Did you hear me about Olivia fucking Kennedy?"

Chuck snorted. "Yeah, I heard you. The dirty bitch almost wrecked your future, but here you are. You beat the odds to walk again. You beat the damn odds to skate again. Now you have the chance to beat the odds a third fucking time and skate for a"—Chuck slowed down to pound out each word like he was driving it home with a sledgehammer—"*professional fucking hockey team.* Fuck it, Keisha. I've told you for years you should go pro. You have the talent."

"Yeah, and what if I get injured again?"

He snorted. "You're playing semi-pro hockey with a bunch of nobodies. There's just as much chance of injury in our games."

"Chuck, you're not a nobody. None of y'all are."

"Thanks, but this is different. You talk about everything Olivia Kennedy almost stole from you. If you don't take this chance then *you* will only be stealing from yourself. And for what? Pride? Fear? Nervousness? Insecurity? Go to Portland and show everyone—*including* this bitch—how Keisha Owens gets shit done on the ice."

"What about our next game?"

Chuck laid a calloused hand on her shoulder. "Keisha, who fucking cares? Let me ask you this? When little Keisha strapped on those skates all those years ago, did she dream of skating with a bunch of broken down has-beens and cocky wanna-bes in a semi-pro league, or did that little girl dream of skating with the best players in the world in a professional league? Maybe even the Olympics?"

She rolled her eyes and kicked at her shoes like she did when her mom lectured her when she was a kid, but she knew Chuck was right. "Okay, yeah. You have a point."

"Then do it. Me and the rest of the Vipers will watch every damn one of your games. We'll cheer you on and tell stories about how you used to be one of us before you hit the big time."

"You do know this is batshit crazy, right? What if I can't cut it?"

Chuck pulled her in for a hug. "I know you've got this, and even if they don't pick you up after the ten-day contract is up, then at least you *know* you gave it your best. Now call the Blossoms back before you overthink this. Or underthink it. *Again.*"

"Fine, but let's go inside. It's cold enough to freeze a moose out here."

"Amen, sister."

Keisha pulled out her phone and dialed the Portland number.

"This is Miles Caine." He added wryly, "Do I need further instruction on how to fuck off?"

"Very funny. I'm in."

"Great. There's a red eye leaving in four hours for Portland. Can you make it?"

"You want me to fly out *tonight?*"

"We have a game in two days. We'd like to do your physical and onboarding tomorrow."

"Y'all don't mess around."

Caine chuckled. "No, we do not, Ms. Owens."

"Send me the info, and I'll be on the plane."

"Wonderful. My assistant will text you the details. See you tomorrow. Do you have an agent?"

Keisha's heart sank. "No."

"If I may dare give you advice, you might want to look into getting one. Good night, Ms. Owens."

"Night." Keisha hung up and walked over to Chuck, grinning like a madwoman. "Come on, I need to pack a few things, and then you're giving me a ride to the airport."

Chapter 4

Mama Weer All Crazy Now
Quiet Riot

Keisha was sitting in the terminal when she finally had a chance to call her mother.

"Hey, baby. Is everything okay?" Tamika yawned, picking up on the third ring. "You're calling late."

"I'm sorry, Mom. I hate to wake you, but I have news. I'm at the airport waiting for a flight to Portland."

"Portland? Oregon?"

She chuckled, "Definitely not the one in Maine." Putting on her serious voice, she continued, "Mom, I'm going to play professional hockey."

Keisha yanked the phone away from her ear as Tamika screeched. *"What? Baby, that's amazing!"*

"It is. But there's a catch." She took a breath, anticipating her mother's reaction. "Olivia Kennedy plays for Portland."

If Tamika was half asleep before, this revelation must have woken her all the way up as Keisha swore she could feel her mother shake with bitter rage through the phone. "Keisha, you know I don't believe in holding grudges"—her mother stopped speaking and Keisha could almost feel the struggle to maintain a motherly tone—"but I have a fierce dislike for that bitch."

"I know, Mom. I turned them down twice before I said yes."

"Why *did* you agree to play on the same damn team as her?"

"Something Chuck said. About not letting her steal my dreams. Mom, I'm going pro, even if I have to go through Olivia to do it. And Portland has been the only team to call me. Now it's on me to shoot my shot."

"I believe in you, baby. And if Olivia Kennedy stands in your way, then take her out. She definitely has it coming."

"Truth."

"I'm proud of you. You travel safe and keep me updated, you hear? I'll be praying for you."

"Thanks, Mom. I love you."

"Love you, too, baby girl."

Keisha called the non-profit she worked at to tell them she would be out for a week or so. She texted Sharon with the news, knowing Sharon wouldn't see it until morning. Leaning back, she pulled out her book and squirmed in the boarding lounge seat.

I swear these seats are some kind of mass psychological experiment in torture. I know—if they make the seats uncomfortable, then passengers will have to get up and walk around, taking them past concessions, which drives up sales. Well, at least I won't fall asleep and miss my flight.

The airplane seat was almost as uncomfortable, but the plane was only about two thirds full, allowing Keisha the luxury of spreading out. The flight was uneventful, as was the ride to the motel. It was cheap and rundown, but close to the coliseum. Keisha had to step over a drunk to get to her room where she caught another couple hours of sleep.

Not a great first impression, Portland.

She arrived at the facility early in the morning. A team staffer walked her through the required paperwork and brought her in to see Miles Caine. He appeared to be in his early forties, wearing an expensive suit with a Blossoms tie. His megawatt smile was wasted on Keisha, but she could sense its genuineness.

"Good morning, Ms. Owens. After our scintillating conversations last night, it's a pleasure to finally meet you."

"Hello, Mr. Caine. Sorry about telling you to fuck yourself. Oh, shit. Am I allowed to swear in front of my boss?"

He chuckled, the far edges of his lips twitching upward. "I'm not your boss until you sign the contract. Seriously though, you may speak freely with me, including expletives."

Keisha's back muscles relaxed, releasing some of her tension. "I have to ask. Why me?"

His lips twitched further upward. "As in, do I know your history with Olivia Kennedy? Or why would I take a chance on a semi-pro player?"

"Both."

"A scout was in Minneapolis to evaluate college talent when he heard some interesting tales about a woman playing on a semi-pro team. He caught a Vipers game and sent me an intriguing report. I've been in the hockey business long enough that I recalled your name. I watched the video from your championship run your junior year. Simply astounding. There are quite a few people in the hockey world who felt you could have been the next Great One were it not for Ms. Kennedy." Caine tilted his head, eyes examining her face. "If you still have half the potential you did back then, you're a game changer. And if you've seen the standings, then you know the Blossoms desperately need a change."

Keisha laughed. "I don't know about the next Great One, but I'm certain you must be crazy desperate to put me in the same room with Olivia Kennedy."

Caine chuckled wryly. "We're dead last in the league. We haven't won a game in weeks. Alicia Bollard, our third leading scorer with a grand total of *two* goals, is out for at least a month with a high ankle sprain. Crazy and desperate fit the bill."

"All right. Where do I sign?"

He slid a sheaf of papers across the desk. "This is a standard ten-day contract. If we do keep you on the team, we will likely do a second ten-day contract while we negotiate a contract with your agent."

"Sounds good." Keisha signed the papers. "What's next?"

"Next is your physical." Caine stood and gestured at the door. "Obviously, if you don't pass, then the contract is null and void, and we'll fly you home at no charge."

I'm glad it was obvious to you. I didn't even think to ask before I upended my life and boarded a plane to fly halfway across the country.

"Obviously..."

"I'll take you to meet our training staff. They're down the hall."

"Thanks."

The team's medical staff gave Keisha a thorough examination, paying particular attention to her old injuries. After the grueling exam and a blood draw for further testing, Keisha was tentatively cleared.

Caine met her at the door and escorted her to the locker room. "The team is already practicing, so you can meet them on the ice when you've changed."

"Sounds good. One question. Is the number sixty-four available?"

"It is. I presume you wish to wear it?"

Keisha's grin showed her teeth. "Oh, heck yes I do."

"You strike me as a woman who has passionate, yet deliberate reasons for her decisions. May I ask if there is a story behind the choice of sixty-four?"

"On July 2, 1964," Keisha explained with a fierce grin. "Lyndon Johnson signed the Civil Rights Act into law."

Caine grinned. "I will have our equipment staff get number sixty-four ready for you immediately."

A member of the training staff met her inside the locker room, fitting her out with pads. Keisha brought her own skates. On the ice wearing a practice jersey, she waved at Caine and a woman she presumed was the coach before skating over to the rest of the team. Keisha tapped number ninety-eight on the shoulder, and punched her square in the face when she turned around.

Chapter 5

Screaming For Vengeance
Judas Priest

Olivia heard her nose pop when the fist slammed into her face. More fists followed as she crumpled to the ice. The shouts of her teammates filled her ears as the blows finally stopped raining down on her face. She felt strong arms lift her and help her skate over to the bench. Someone handed her a towel, which she used to wipe away the tears and blood in her eyes.

Coach Hicks turned to Miles Caine and remarked with unmistakable sarcasm, "Well, she certainly knows how to make a great first impression."

Looking left, Olivia saw Cruz and Schmidt restraining an apoplectic Black woman, who screamed, "That's right, *bitch.* How's it feel to get blind-sided, you fucking coward?"

Oh, fuck. It's Keisha Owens.

Turning back to Caine and Hicks, Olivia demanded, "What the hell is she doing here?"

Caine responded evenly, "Let me remind you that I make personnel decisions for this team. Bollard is out, so we signed Keisha Owens to a ten-day contract." His brows furrowed as he glared at the two players. "Since we've now gotten the introductions out of the way, I trust the two of you will handle yourselves professionally going forward."

Keisha replied with a lopsided grin as she broke free of the two defenders and smoothed down her jersey, "You got it, boss. So long as the Puck Princess stays out of my way."

Olivia spat blood into her towel. "I was assaulted." Pointing at Keisha, Olivia shrieked, "She is a goddamn menace. You can't be serious about this."

"All yours, coach." Caine patted Hicks on the shoulder as he turned toward the exit.

Hicks grimaced and rolled her eyes before pitching her voice for the entire rink to hear. "There's too much nervous energy out here. I want everyone doing wind sprints down and back until I tell you to stop. First one to puke owes me fifty burpees."

The team gave a collective groan before starting to skate.

"Faster. I want to see you sweat," Hicks roared.

Miller broke first, her pink hair clinging damply to her neck as she vomited into the trash can at the bench.

Olivia joined the rest of the team around Coach Hicks. Her chest heaved as her lungs grasped urgently for air. She made sure to keep a safe distance away from Keisha in case the other woman decided to attack her again. The sounds of Miller crying as she vomited again could be heard over the team's heavy breathing.

Hicks looked over the team with a stern expression. "Are we done with stupid shit?" No one had the lung capacity to answer the rhetorical question. "I'll take your collective silence as an affirmative. Since there are no comments, we're going to run drills in the lines for tomorrow night's game. Top line is Thomas, Jensen, and LeBeau. Second line is Rose, Cartwright, and Dvorak. Third line is Bouchard, Gagne, and Hall. Fourth line is Kennedy, Owens, and Miller."

Fourth line? I've been demoted to the fucking fourth line on the worst team in the league. If I ever needed a flashing neon sign saying that my career is over, then this is it.

"Uh, coach—"

Olivia's teeth clicked shut as the coach's head whipped around and her furious glare melted any further protest. Satisfied by the silence, Hicks turned and barked at Cathy as she returned to the ice, wiping her mouth. "You owe me fifty burpees before practice tomorrow, Miller."

The pink-haired young woman nodded wearily as she skated up to Olivia. "Wanna tell me what's going on?"

Keisha skated up, glowering at Olivia. "Yeah. Do you want to tell her what a weak-ass bitch you are, or should I?"

"I wasn't so weak when I put you in the hospital."

Keisha drew her arm back to throw another punch, but Heike caught her fist before she could swing. Daniella skated between the two, nudging them away from each other.

"I'm not doing more wind sprints because of you *putas*," Daniella growled. "You two are going to get your shit together for the next hour, or Heike and I will *personally* ensure that your issues are no longer everyone else's problem. *Comprende?*"

Hicks called from the bench, "Is there a book club meeting, or are you here to practice?"

Olivia shook her head. "Fine. Let's do this before *someone* gets the team into more trouble." She cradled a puck on the blade of her stick before flipping it into the air. When the puck hit the ice, she passed it to Cathy. Daniella and Heike stayed with the fourth line as they ran their drills.

I hate having Cruz and Schmidt hanging around like babysitters, but if it keeps the peace, then I guess I'll deal. It's certainly better than having a maniac assaulting me. Whatever possessed Caine to bring that woman to Portland? She obviously took the contract so she could exact revenge on me.

She did her best to bury herself in the routine and ignore the air of uncertainty around her. Oddly, Olivia felt better during practice than she had in a while.

I'm pretty sure this is what rock bottom feels like. I might as well have fun while I'm here. There's only two ways for my career to go now—up or out.

Daniella and Heike shadowed Olivia and Keisha in the locker room, silently enforcing the truce. In the film room, Olivia was left alone with Cathy and Keisha as they watched tape of Boston while Hicks discussed strategy and what to look for against their upcoming opponent.

Olivia fully expected Keisha to try something in the darkness, but instead noted the other woman's eyes glued to the screen. As Hicks was wrapping up, Keisha spoke up. "Hey, coach. I noticed something."

Heads turned throughout the room. "What is it, Owens?"

"When Boston is on the rush, Turner likes to pinch up and in from her left D spot. I feel like there's an opportunity for a quick right wing like Miller to get a jump in the other direction. The feed might be tricky to beat Turner, but there's a good opportunity for a breakaway there."

Hicks raised her eyebrows. "Good eye, Owens. I'll take a look." She surveyed the room. "All right, we are done for today. We have light practice at the training facility in the morning. I will see you then."

Daniella fell in beside Olivia as they left, escorting her out while Heike did the same with Keisha. Olivia felt a growing itch between her shoulder blades as the normally loquacious defender trudged next to her in silence. Outside, Daniella caught her arm. "I watched the video of what you did to Keisha. *Holy shit.* I don't think I've ever seen such a dirty fucking hit, *puta.* You deserved the ass-kicking she gave you today, and more. The only reason I'm here right now is because I don't want to do any more damn wind sprints. As far as Heike and I are concerned, once you're off these grounds, Keisha has every right to beat your ass like a drum." Daniella punctuated her rant by spitting loudly at Olivia's feet.

Too ashamed to respond, Olivia walked quickly away, eyes searching every shadow for an ambush. She knew the truth of

Daniella's words. Whatever revenge Keisha exacted now could never make up for what Olivia had stolen from her twelve years ago. She breathed a sigh of relief when she closed the door to her apartment.

Collapsing on the couch, she posted some shots from her latest modeling gig on social media, mostly to remind her fiancé she was still alive. Their wedding was eight months away and preparations were moving slowly. Probably because Maxim spent so much of his time being photographed with clingy models and giddy puck bunnies, often with his hand planted firmly on their asses.

He doesn't have the faintest concept of discretion. I'll remind him when we're both in Vancouver. Of course, no thought lasts long in his thick skull. Marrying Maxim makes my parents happy, though, and right now, I'm thrilled for anything to get them off my back. Plus, as much as Maxim is a pain in my ass, at least I lived in a sweet condo instead of a shithole like this. I didn't have to worry about money, either. I'm not sure how I'm going to cover rent this month and still make a dent in the mountain of credit card bills.

She stood up and made her way to the bathroom. Looking at her bruised face in the mirror, Olivia felt glad she didn't have any modeling shoots for the foreseeable future. As it was, she wasn't sure how she would be able to cover up the bruises and cuts.

Lost in her dour thoughts, Olivia fixed herself a miserable and lonely dinner before going online to buy three new dresses. She maxed out another credit card to complete the transaction, but the endorphin rush of making the purchase soothed her slightly before she drifted off into troubled sleep.

Chapter 6

I Gotta Feeling

Black Eyed Peas

The rumble of traffic woke Keisha before her alarm did. Exhaustion was the only reason she managed to get to sleep in spite of the uncomfortable bed and incessant train whistles from the depot down by the Willamette. Her phone dinged as she exited the shower with a message from Heike asking her to meet for breakfast.

Keisha pulled on her coat before exiting into the moist, gray Portland morning. The Rose City wasn't nearly as cold as the Twin Cities, but the dampness crawled into her bones. Thankfully, the walk to the breakfast place wasn't far. She waved at the towering German brunette, who was unsurprisingly accompanied by the raven-tressed Daniella. The two defenders waved back and greeted Keisha with hugs.

"Good morning. I wasn't expecting hugs after yesterday. Between wind sprints and punching your teammate, I thought y'all would hate me."

Heike shrugged. "We saw the video. Plus, Olivia has a *backpfeifengesicht,* so how could we blame you?"

Keisha shook her head. "I'm sorry, what?"

"A punchable face."

They all snickered and Keisha nodded her head. "Her face is very punchable."

Once they ordered, Daniella asked, "What's the deal with you two?"

"Besides her nearly disabling me?"

"Yeah. Olivia is a whiny bitch and a half-assed player, but even she wouldn't hit someone like she did over a bad game. There must be some history between the two of you."

Keisha related the story of her first run-in with the Puck Princess, as well as their subsequent meetings, where Keisha's inner city team was humiliated and mocked, right up to her junior year and the fateful championship game. She detailed her team's Cinderella run through the state tournament right to the penultimate moment. Keisha's eyes watered as she spoke about the aftermath of relearning how to walk and skate.

Daniella and Heike's faces were flushed with anger by the end of Keisha's tale. "What are you going to do about it?" Daniella growled.

As her anger coursed through well-worn ruts in her mind, Keisha leaned back in her as her mind struggled to process the question. "I honestly don't know. I've dreamed about cutting Olivia Kennedy down to size for years now, but everything has always been in the realm of the theoretical. Obviously, punching her felt great, but I'm not sure what else I can do to her. The bitch's career is on life-support. She's not on the international roster anymore..."

"There's one thing you can do," Heike said, a wicked grin spreading across her face as she leaned forward on her elbows. "Be better than her. *Again.*"

Keisha whistled. "Beating the brat on the ice is fitting. Doesn't feel quite as viscerally good as punching her, though."

Heike chuckled while Daniella threw her head back and roared.

"Hey, thank you both for inviting me to breakfast and being cool."

The pretty Latina grinned. "Our pleasure. Since we're friends now, my brother Sebastian is in town, and my parents keep bugging me to find him a nice *American* girl..."

Keisha snickered. "Sorry. He's *definitely* not my type."

"Oh, because..." Daniella made a penis-like motion with her finger.

"Yep. I don't like sausage. I'm more of a boxed lunch kind of girl." Keisha giggled.

"Damn. Too bad for my parents, I guess." She reached out to take the hand of the tall German. "We like you, but Heike and I are...complicated. By the way, all my friends call me Dani. We're friends now, right?"

"Thank you. And yes, we're friends. Also, what does 'complicated' mean?"

"It's a very long story."

"I keep telling you, stop cockblocking Sebastian and Svetlana," Heike added. "He's completely hung up on her."

"He's too short. She'd never go for it over the long term," Dani countered.

"I might be the new girl here, but maybe be cool with your brother and Svetlana going on some dates, and then see what *they* think."

Dani sighed. "Fine. But if they become an item, she better not bring borscht to family dinner. What the hell is borscht anyway?"

Heike and Keisha teased Dani all throughout the drive to the practice facility. Coach Hicks met them outside the locker room. "You three, with me." They exchanged glances as they followed her to the film room. "Owens, good eye. Now I want you to watch this compilation. In practice today, Cruz, I want you to mimic what Turner is doing. Then we're going to practice exploiting it."

"Got it, coach."

They practiced a lot during the morning session, but the team struggled to get the puck past Dani. Everyone tapped Dani's pads to show their respect as they exited the ice on the way to the locker room.

Keisha decided to explore Portland while she had the chance as a way to unwind before tonight's game. Given the miserable weather, she decided the best place to explore was Powell's Books. She spent hours inside browsing happily, limiting herself to a few choices given her budgetary constraints.

The locker room was tense before the game. A loss or tie tonight would bring their winless streak to ten. Keisha hadn't been part of her new team's slide, but she had friends now who she wanted to spare the ignominy of such a wretched mark.

Portland was already down one goal by the time the fourth line saw its first shift. They were up against Boston's second line, mostly playing defense in their own zone. Keisha patrolled her left wing while Cathy and a defender scrapped for the puck in the far corner. Cathy managed to win the board battle and pass back to a Blossoms defender behind the net. Keisha and Olivia surged forward, forcing Boston back at the blue line. A quick pass from behind the net got the puck to Cathy, who slid it forward to Olivia in neutral ice. Olivia deked a defender, drifting into the right circle. She passed across the middle, just beyond Keisha's reach. A Boston winger, trailing the play, corralled the puck, sending it up ice just as Keisha checked her. Portland's fourth line went for a change, replaced by the top line.

On the bench, Keisha grabbed hold of Olivia's face guard. "Were you intentionally passing to the other team, or do you just not want me to have the puck? I had the shot."

"It was a perfect pass. Maybe try not to be so damn slow next time."

"Huh. Whose fault is it that I'm not as fast as I used to be?" Keisha felt her blood boiling as her fingers twisted in the cage on Olivia's helmet. The other woman batted ineffectually at Keisha's arm.

Two hands came down to nudge them apart. Hicks hissed, "Would you like to do burpees on skates for the entire intermission?" The coach studied their faces before answering her own rhetorical question. "No? Then get your shit together because you're on in two shifts."

Their next shift brought Keisha what promised to be lovely bruises as she blocked two shots with her body. The fourth line was on the ice for nearly two minutes before they managed to clear the puck out of their zone.

In the locker room at the first intermission, Hicks had some suggestions for how the top line could work to beat the stifling Boston defense. For the other three lines, the coach critiqued their defensive play and exhorted them to loosen up on offense. She heaped praise on Svetlana, who only allowed one goal despite facing fifteen shots.

Back for the second period, Boston caught the second line out of position and scored on a three-two rush. Keisha felt Hicks' icy fury radiating as the coach paced behind her.

I have to respect a coach who isn't losing her shit right about now. She's doing her best to keep up morale, even though we are completely shitting the bed.

Almost midway through the second period, the fourth line got its first ice time. Gagne dumped the puck into the offensive zone as Portland went for a full change. Keisha caught a Boston defender in the corner, fighting viciously for the puck. Wresting control, Keisha flipped the puck back to the blue line where the defender, Radokova, took a low percentage shot. Cathy collected the rebound, cycling it to Olivia behind the net as Keisha slid into the slot.

"*Kennedy. Here,*" Keisha barked. Positioned as she was, Keisha drew two defenders. Olivia didn't have a clear pass, so she skated behind the net with another Boston player hounding her. Their gaze met, and Keisha flicked her eyes to the other side of the crease where Cathy drifted in unmarked. She banged her stick on the ice, keeping

Boston focused on her when Olivia backhanded a no-look pass to Cathy, who buried the puck in the back of the twine.

Red lights flashed and sirens blared as the arena erupted in cheers. Keisha and Olivia both reached Cathy at the same time, wrapping her in a double bear hug, quickly joined by the defenders. They were met with fist bumps along the bench. Amidst the accolades for Cathy's first professional goal, Keisha sat down and collected herself on the bench when Coach Hicks leaned in to whisper in her ear, "Congratulations on your first professional point."

She turned her head to respond and instead found herself staring at Olivia. "Nice fucking pass," Keisha blurted.

"Thanks. And thank you for the heads up. Good work."

Suddenly feeling awkward, Keisha turned back to watch the action resume on the ice. It felt strange exchanging civil words with Olivia.

Two shifts later, Boston scored on a power play, bringing the deficit back to two. Keisha could feel Hicks' tension behind her. "Cruz. Schmidt. Are you two good?" Hicks barked. When they nodded, she ordered, "Okay. You're up next with the fourth line."

Keisha focused on Olivia as she bent down to take the face-off at center ice. After a brief scrabble for control, Olivia won the puck back to Heike, who passed it up to Keisha. Keisha stickhandled her way across the blue line before dumping the puck in. Olivia collected the puck, skating to the left side behind the net. Keisha planted herself in front of the crease, resisting any attempts to jostle her out of the way. Olivia passed back to the blue line where Heike ripped off a howling slap shot. The goalie had no chance to react because of Keisha's screen and the sirens went off again.

Back on the bench again, Keisha once more said, "Nice fucking pass."

"Way to set the screen."

"Thanks."

This feels really weird. Just normal banter with my teammates, but this is Olivia fucking Kennedy, and nothing with her is normal.

The atmosphere in the locker room at the second intermission was buzzing. The Blossoms were still down one, but the team had life now. Keisha's line took the ice following the third line, suddenly facing Boston's top line. Boston's best bore down on the rush. Just as she observed on game film, Keisha saw Turner pinching in.

"Miller, ready," Keisha bellowed just before Heike leveled Boston's right wing against the boards in the corner. The puck popped loose and Heike flipped it to Keisha, who saucered it up and over so the disc caromed off the side boards to an accelerating Cathy. She collected the puck at center ice, breaking past Turner, who desperately flailed for a hook on the speeding winger. Cathy raced toward the net, forcing the goalie to commit to a forehand feint, before sliding the puck to the other side for an easy backhand goal. The next shift, Misty Thomas found Karla Jensen for the go-ahead goal.

Portland held on for a 4-3 win, snapping their month-long winless streak. Keisha grinned as she skated back onto the ice and waved to the crowd as she collected the game's third star.

The locker room was bedlam when Keisha walked in. Cathy ran up and hugged her hard before returning to her cubby. Coach Hicks walked in and blew her whistle. "Congratulations on the win tonight. There is a *lot* of room for improvement. I'd like a win where Kravchenko doesn't have to make forty-three saves. But we'll work on defense in practice," she said with an evil grin. "Of course, I have to mention Miller with her first two professional goals, and Owens for your first two professional assists. We surprised Boston tonight, but we can't expect to catch our next opponent sleeping."

Chapter 7

Only The Lonely
The Motels

Olivia felt amazing, elated, and deeply conflicted. In the moment—out in the arena—everything was perfect. Now, as her team celebrated around her, things were murky and complicated. She couldn't remember the last time she saw the ice like she did tonight. Her no-look pass on the first goal was magic—as if she could sense Cathy's position in the slot. Olivia looked across the room at Keisha, and touched her face, feeling the bruises there.

On the ice, she could think of Keisha as a jersey and a number. A stick to pass a puck to. Off the ice, Olivia was frankly terrified at what the other woman might do to her. The team was going out to celebrate tonight, but Olivia was leery about being in a social situation with someone who attacked her the day before. She could call the beating unprovoked, but deep down she knew she had it coming.

Olivia surveyed the room again, observing her teammates laughing and congratulating each other. Something about their interactions nagged at her mind until she finally made the connection—no one was talking with her. Olivia stood up and stepped over to the clump of people chatting with Schmidt. "Amazing shot on your goal, Heike."

"Thanks," she replied tersely.

Heike said nothing else, returning to her conversation like Olivia wasn't even there. The same interaction played out when she congratulated Svetlana. Olivia didn't dare engage with Keisha, so she mingled with the cluster around Cathy instead. "Congratulations on your first two professional goals. You had a phenomenal night."

"Thanks, Olivia. I couldn't have done it without amazing assists from you and Keisha."

Olivia winced at her rival's name but smiled through the discomfort. "Your feint on the second goal was perfect. Their goalie never stood a chance."

The pink-haired woman clapped her hands gleefully. "I know. I practice my feints on Svetlana all the time, but I usually struggle with the timing. Tonight, everything clicked, and I got it perfect."

"Yeah, you did." Olivia punctuated her praise with a friendly hand on the shoulder.

"Speaking of perfection. Your no-look pass on my first goal was out of this world."

Olivia noted the cluster of players around Cathy had all drifted off to join the other groups. Icy cold realization flooded her veins. *They know. I can see it in their glances. They all know what I did, and they hate me for it.* She plastered a smile across her face as she responded, "Owens alerted me, and I just flicked the puck back to where you would probably be. I'm just glad you were in the right place."

"She's so smart. Her realization about Turner's positioning got me the second goal."

Olivia sighed. "Yeah. She is." When Cathy didn't say anything more, Olivia decided to ask the question burning in her mind. "You know, don't you? Everyone knows."

Cathy's face flushed to match her hair. "I mean, we've all seen the video. But Keisha told Dani and Heike the full story about everything else before the hit, and now we all know."

Anger mixed with guilt and shame in her mind. She wanted to lash out. She wanted to crawl into a hole and hide. Instead, Olivia asked the obvious question, "Why are you talking with me?"

The younger woman considered the question. "Because sometimes people do stupid things. Especially when they're young." Cathy looked at her toes. "I know you don't like me, but I make it a goal to get to know all of my teammates."

Olivia hadn't thought it was possible to feel even more guilty, but Cathy's words dumped a truckload of additional shame on her. "I…" She paused before she lied, choosing instead to speak truthfully. "Cathy, hear me out, okay? When we first met, I found you immensely irritating. My irritation wasn't your fault. It was entirely mine. I've been in a bad place emotionally for a long time, and you're just so eager and friendly…my reaction to you wasn't fair. I'm truly sorry for being a judgy bitch and not giving you a chance. I do like you."

"Thank you for being honest. If I can be truthful in return, I'm struggling with how to think about you." She looked up from her toes and struck a lopsided grin. "It was easier when you were being a bitch all the time."

Somehow, Olivia felt even guiltier. "I could go back to the whole bitchy ice queen thing."

Cathy giggled. "Please don't."

Olivia sighed. "It might be better for you. You're young and don't need the stain of associating with me following you around."

"Don't say such things. Come on. Get changed, and let's go hang out with the team."

Thirty minutes later, Olivia found herself crammed against the wall of the Sports Bra, a sports bar dedicated to women's sports. The place was packed, but she felt completely alone. Daniella came in late, dragging a man behind her. Olivia watched as they walked up to Svetlana. Daniella pushed the guy in front of the towering Russian and left. Olivia's eyes followed her as she stalked over to where Heike was enthusiastically tongue-wrestling some guy. Daniella tapped Heike on the shoulder to interrupt the kiss, then proceeded to grab the guy's face and kiss him before kissing her blue line partner. *Well, that's interesting,* Olivia said to herself.

Taking another awkward sip of her beer, Olivia felt a tap on her shoulder. She turned to look into Cathy's smiling face framed by her pink locks. "Do you have glitter on your face?"

Cathy brought her hand up to reflexively tap her cheek. "Yeah. I like it. Do you want some?"

"Uh."

"Come on, live a little, Liv." The young woman's enthusiasm washed in with the inexorable force of the tides.

"Did you just call me, Liv?"

"Are you okay with a nickname? I thought it was cute."

"No one calls me cute. Or Liv."

"Oh."

The disappointment on Cathy's face made Olivia feel like she just kicked a puppy. "You know what. You can call me Liv." The other woman's face lit up. Olivia sighed. "And cute, too. Although I feel like I'm well past the point of being cute."

"Aw, don't sell yourself short, Liv. You're definitely cute. Super pretty, too."

"Uh, you're not hitting on me, are you?"

Cathy roared, wiping tears away.

"Wow. You don't have to laugh so hard about it."

The other woman collected herself. "Liv, you're too funny. No, I'm not into girls, but if I were, then I'd totally hit on you. You're super hot." Cathy paused. "Do you mind if I ask, what's going on with you and what's his name? Kovalev?"

"We're getting married, why?"

"Like, I know you're engaged and all, but..."

Olivia raised her eyebrows. "But?"

"I mean, I never met him or anything, but I guess I worry about how he treats you. All the tabloid stuff—it's not right."

"Maxim and I are none of your business," Olivia hissed.

"I know. I'm sorry. It's just that I like you and don't want to see you get hurt."

Olivia's shoulders relaxed and her eyebrows unknitted. "Thank you, Cathy. I'm sorry I snapped at you. Like I said before, I've been in a bad place for a while."

Her mercurial companion cheered back up. "We need to get you in a better frame of mind. Wanna come do yoga with me?"

"Yoga? Sure."

Cathy squealed. "Oh my gosh, I'm so excited. Give me your phone number so I can text you the details." Olivia handed over her phone. "This will be so much fun." The pink-haired pixie bounced giddily.

"No one wanted to do yoga with you before?"

"I think I might have scared them off."

Olivia chuckled. "You are super enthusiastic about this."

Cathy gave her a pixie-like grin. "I know, right?" She handed back Olivia's phone, then began typing rapidly on her own phone. Cathy bit her lower lip as her fingers flew. Even Olivia had to admit she was adorable.

"Okay. Sent."

Olivia checked her phone. "Ugh. You know this is right before practice?"

Another happy squeal. "I know. It's such a good workout, and then you feel amazing on the ice. You'll love it, I promise."

"Uh-huh." Olivia knew she sounded skeptical, but Cathy didn't notice. "Well, I'm gonna finish my beer and head home. I need a good night's sleep if I'm going to survive early morning yoga *and* practice."

"Okay. See you tomorrow." Cathy waved at her as she left before plunging into the crowd of Blossoms.

Olivia went home to her cheap apartment, tossed her keys on the table and collapsed on her bed. *How sad is it that Cathy is the closest thing to a friend I have right now?* She checked her phone one more time to see if there were any messages from her parents. Nothing. She did have a voicemail from her brother, Patrick.

Her brother's voice sounded a bit tinny through the speaker, but just hearing him was comforting. "Great job tonight, Livvy. Bruce and I thought you looked amazing. Um, not to be weird, but are you skating on the same line as the girl you put in the hospital? *Awkward.* Anyway, call me back when you get this. *Kisses.*"

Lying back on her bed, Olivia debated calling Patrick. She needed sleep, but she also needed family.

"Hey, Pat."

"Hi, Livvy. So, was I imagining things, or are you linemates with your old rival?"

"Ugh. That's your first question?"

"Bitch, please. Of course it is. We'll get to you once you give me the tea."

"Fine. Yes, I'm skating with Keisha Owens. I didn't know she was on the team until she smashed a fist into my face."

"Oh…" Patrick sucked in his breath. She could hear his grimace of familial pain, even if she couldn't see it. "Ow. I'm sorry, Livvy. Are you all right?"

She sighed. "Yeah. No. I have bruises all over. She punches hard."

"So she just suckerpunched you?"

"Yeah."

"Not to be an asshole, but you definitely had it coming..."

Olivia sighed again, louder. "I know. I'm still not a fan of being repeatedly punched in the face."

"Ouch. And then your coach put you two on the same line? Is she batshit crazy, or completely off her rocker?"

Olivia laughed, and tiny tingles reminded her of her bruises again. "Crazy like a fox. Out on the ice...Pat...I can't describe it. The first period was rocky, but then everything clicked. I haven't felt like I could see the ice like that in forever. Not just see it. I could *feel* it."

"I know, Livvy. Your no look pass...it reminded me of how we used to play when we were kids." She could hear the awe in her older brother's voice.

"Exactly. I had fun playing hockey for the first time in years. And then the game ended and everything is shit again. Well, not everything. I might have made a friend."

Her brother gasped theatrically. "Do tell. Please tell me he's hot and you're going to ditch your moron fiancé."

"*She* is Cathy Miller, my right wing. Super nice and far too energetic. Before you ask, yes, she's straight, and I'm still straight, too."

"Boo. You'd be an incredible lesbian...or bisexual, whatever. Plus, I hate being the only disappointment in the family."

"Oh, you're not the only one. Mom and Dad barely speak to me."

"Even after a two point night?" Her brother's voice cracked, betraying his resentment of their parents on her behalf.

"Nothing."

"They're such *dicks*, Livvy. I still love you." He paused. "Bruce loves you, too. He also concurs about you making an incredible lesbian."

"Thanks, guys. Okay, I need sleep. Cathy and I are doing yoga in the morning."

"*Ohh.*"

"Hush, Pat. I love you. Good night."

"Night, Livvy. Love you."

Olivia put her phone down.

Tonight was a good night.

Chapter 8

(We Are) The Roadcrew
Motörhead

Keisha didn't stay at the bar for long. Dani and Heike were passing some dude back and forth between them and clearly weren't in a talking mood. Keisha wanted to chat with Cathy, but Cathy was talking with Olivia fucking Kennedy. At least the drink was free, a reward for scoring three points in her debut game. She stayed long enough to be polite before making her way back to her crappy motel room.

Lying in bed, Keisha pulled up the videos for Chicago's recent games, studying their play. She woke up the next morning and did more film study in a local coffee shop while eating two breakfast sandwiches. Refueled after last night's exertions, she went to practice. Coach rewarded their win with light drills. About halfway through practice, Hicks called the fourth line over to the bench.

"Good job yesterday netting three points for us."

"Thanks, Coach," the trio said in unison.

"Don't thank me yet. Miller, I need you to be more aggressive on offense. If Owens is in the corner and Kennedy's along the boards, then I need you in the slot to grab a loose puck or provide a screen for the defenders."

Hicks focused on Olivia next. "Kennedy, what the hell was that garbage pass in the first? I know you can do better."

"It's not my fault, coach. She's just too slow." Olivia punctuated her complaint by pointing her thumb at Keisha.

"*My fault?* I'm not as fast as I used to be because someone broke my damn leg. Huh, I wonder who?" Keisha ground out through clenched teeth. Her blood was boiling.

Hicks stepped between the two before fists flew. "She's right, Owens. You're too damn slow. I saw it during sprints and in the game."

"Coach..."

"*Ah.*" Hicks held up a hand. "So we're going to work on your speed today." A vicious grin spread from ear to ear. "So, today only, you get *one* free punch on Kennedy—"

"*What?*" Olivia shrieked.

"—but you have to catch her first."

Keisha showed her teeth. "Hell, yeah."

"Kennedy, I'm giving you a three count headstart. One, two..." Olivia dropped her stick and fled. "Three. Go get her."

Keisha took off after the fleeing center, her eyes locked onto the number ninety-eight on Olivia's back. *A free revenge punch is worth chasing the bitch all the way to Seattle if I have to.* Her pursuit was relentless, yet Olivia kept out of reach. *Bitch is fast, but I'll get her.* Keisha's legs were burning as she tracked Olivia from one end of the ice to the other. Her quarry dodged and weaved through the other players, always just out of reach.

Gray haze seeped into her vision, and her lungs were on fire when a blaring whistle finally cut through the fog in her mind. "Owens, to the bench." When she didn't fall back, Hicks barked, *"Owens. Now."* Keisha reluctantly broke off her pursuit and wheeled toward the bench. Her legs felt like rubber, and she gratefully caught the boards before she collapsed.

"Kennedy. Get over here." Hicks tapped Keisha on the shoulder. "Your free pass just expired." Keisha nodded wearily, but she let a smirk crawl onto her lips. She might have missed her chance to throw a free punch, but the Puck Princess still ran like a frightened rabbit.

Hicks addressed them as their lungs slowed down. "Well, Owens, judging by this little exercise, you are fast. You just needed motivation. Kennedy, remember how to dodge the next time someone lines you up for a check. Now, both of you go see the training staff. I want to make sure you two didn't hurt anything except your egos today."

The training staff fussed over Keisha, scolding her about the danger of overexerting herself, but she only half paid attention. *I'm fast again. I was before, but I've been up in my own head for so long, I never let myself take off the figurative training wheels. Damn, it feels good.*

Sitting next to Cathy in the film room, Keisha felt the pink-haired winger elbow her.

"Owens, are you with us?" Hicks asked.

"Sorry, coach."

"Just wondering if you have any insights for us this time?"

"Oh, right. Chicago likes to play a one-three-one trap, but Hazlett is too aggressive to the outside and almost always takes an extra step before turning, giving a fast left winger an opening. Pressing her will force the deep defender up, opening up space in the center. It's an opportunity to either force a penalty or generate an odd man rush."

Hicks arched an eyebrow. "Seriously?"

"Yeah. Hazlett has played hyper-aggressively since college. It's why she's so dangerous on offense. Defensively, she isn't suited for the trap."

Hicks nodded. "I've been focused on stopping her on offense. Good eye, Owens. All right, people. Regular practice tomorrow before we face off against Chicago. We will travel to Detroit the next afternoon. We have a big hole to climb out of if we're going to save this season. Dismissed."

Keisha stood up and thanked Cathy for saving her. Before she could leave, Hicks barked, "Cruz, Owens. Stay a minute." When the three were alone, Hicks asked, "Cruz, are you still with the same agent?"

"Yes, coach."

"You think she'd take Owens on?"

"I can check with her. Coach, can I ask why?"

Hicks snickered. "Because she's a giant pain in Caine's ass, and she'll get Owens a good deal."

Dani grinned. "I'll call her now."

"Good, now you two get out of here."

Keisha spoke with Dani's agent and agreed to sign on with her. After two hours in the weight room, she went up to the Hoyt Arboretum and spent an hour walking through the trees. It was cold, and at five hundred feet of elevation, the rain was mixed with snow, but it wasn't quite cold enough to stick to the ground.

Back in her motel room, Keisha flipped through a LGBTQ+ dating app to find companionship for the evening. She found a match named Carissa who was willing to meet for Thai and maybe more. Jeans and a Blossoms t-shirt wasn't exactly "fuck me" wear, but it was the best she had. The restaurant was on Broadway, about a mile away. A quick bus ride took Keisha almost door-to-door, which made her happy to avoid the miserably dank Portland night. She ended up waiting an awkward fifteen minutes before Carissa arrived, looking dressed to kill in a black dress and tights.

"Hi. You must be Keisha."

"Heya. Nice to meet you. I feel woefully underdressed."

The pretty brunette laughed. "And I feel overdressed. Why don't we get a table and talk about our clothing choices?"

"Sounds good."

Keisha ordered the Pad See Ew, extra chicken and hot, while Carissa ordered a tofu stir fry, mildly spiced. Carissa started the conversation by asking, "What are the Blossoms?"

"It's Portland's professional hockey team. I'm one of the players."

Carissa's eyes widened in surprise. "No shit. I knew women played hockey because of the Olympics, but I had no clue about Portland having a team. Are you any good?"

Keisha chuckled, certain this was going to be a one-night-stand at best. "I just joined the team, and it's currently last in the league, but we won the first game I played in."

"*Wow.* You're so cool. You must like the team a lot since you wear the shirt."

"Actually, I live in Minneapolis. I'm here on a short-term contract, although maybe I'm about to get a full-year deal. Either way, I didn't pack much. Honestly, it's a clean shirt, so that's why I wore it. Your dress, though...*damn.*"

"Thank you. It was the first thing I grabbed." They both pretended this wasn't a lie.

They chatted agreeably until the food arrived. Keisha devoured her Pad See Ew, savoring the spices as they fired up her taste buds. As much as she liked rice, those big thick noodles made her happy.

Carissa was visibly impressed by Keisha's use of chopsticks, her gaze following the movements. "I never figured out how to use those, so I always ask for a fork."

"It's all in the fingers." Keisha grinned lecherously. "And I'm *very* good with my fingers."

The brunette coughed, then waved for the waitress. "Check, please."

Keisha woke up in the middle of the night in a strange but far more comfortable bed. She stared at the ceiling for a while, listening to Carissa snore next to her. Smiling, she rolled over and went back to sleep.

Chapter 9

Mama Said Knock You Out

LL Cool J

Olivia looked at her phone one last time before stowing it in her cubby. She had a good luck message from Pat, but still nothing from her parents. Maxim's messages had been perfunctory at best. With their busy schedules, she hadn't seen him in almost a month, which made her nervous. In the pre-game meeting, Coach Hicks announced a change in the rotation to get the fourth line more ice time. Olivia welcomed the prospect of more playing time as a way to potentially move back up to the third line.

Sitting on the bench, she felt a hand smack the back of her helmet. She whipped her head around to see Keisha glaring at her.

"Bitch, get your head in the game. We're the next shift."

Olivia retorted, "I'm ready. Keep your damn hands off me."

Cathy did her best to calm the situation. "Hey. Save it for Chicago."

Chicago dumped the puck, and both teams went for a change. Olivia clambered over the boards, seeing Chicago's top line do the same. Chicago came on aggressively, battling for possession along the boards behind the Blossoms net. Heike narrowly won the puck, flipping it to Olivia. Olivia passed backward to Daniella, and Chicago began to fall back into their trap defense. Olivia charged forward, taking the feed from Daniella and immediately pitching the puck forward to Keisha, who blazed past Hazlett. Keisha bounced the puck off the boards and avoided the back defender, collecting it again on the run. She drew the attention of the goalie and the remaining defender, leaving Olivia an open lane on the other side of the slot. Keisha faked a shot, freezing the goalie and forcing the Chicago defender to try a block. A perfect backhand pass put the puck right on the tape of Olivia's stick, and a quick flick of the wrist later, the lamp was lit.

Olivia was crushed against the boards by her teammates as the crowd went wild on the other side of the glass, cheering and banging on the plexiglass. A young child, probably around seven, gazed at her adoringly, a hand drawn sign clutched in her hands.

Her first goal of the season lifted a weight off her shoulders that Olivia hadn't realized was there. Skating back to the bench, Olivia basked in the glow of the goal. She even fist-bumped Keisha before they both realized what they were doing. Her line got three more shifts before the Blossoms went into the first intermission up one goal to zero.

Hicks poured cold water on the team's emotions during the break. "We have forty more minutes of hockey. We're only up by one. Stay focused." Her words didn't have the intended impact as Misty Thomas picked up a penalty early in the second. The penalty was almost killed when Dvorak hooked a Chicago forward. The Blossoms survived a few seconds of five-on-three, then another two minutes of Chicago power play when Portland got called for boarding. The bench collectively groaned as they went back on the penalty kill.

A minute into the third penalty, an exhausted Gagne managed to clear the puck down the ice. Hicks called out, "Cruz, Schmidt, Kennedy, Owens. You're next." The fresh penalty killers boiled over the boards to face Chicago's onslaught. Chicago moved the puck efficiently until they had Portland spread a bit. Olivia dropped to the ice to block a blistering slap shot from the blue line, feeling the sting on her thigh. The puck caromed off her leg where another Chicago player took a shot. Svetlana flicked the puck away as Olivia recovered. Heike collected it and passed forward to Keisha, who flipped it off her stick and over the blue line. Olivia accelerated up the ice as Keisha shouldered past a defender. Olivia's eyes narrowed as she recognized the two-on-one. She altered her trajectory to her right, aiming for the slot. Keisha made a perfect tape-to-tape pass just under the defender's stick. Olivia had a shot, but with the goalie square on, she knew her percentage was low. Instead, she feinted, and passed back across the crease to Keisha, who buried the puck in the twine.

The jailbreak goal emptied the penalty box and sent the crowd into deafening bedlam. Olivia once again found herself face to face with Keisha as they celebrated the point, Heike and Daniella piled onto them, and all four crashed to the ice. Skating back to the bench, Olivia and Keisha were hailed by the rest of the team. There was no fist bump this time, just a brief mutual nod as Cathy wrapped her arms around their shoulders.

"Oh my goodness. You two are amazing," their linemate gushed. "You both got your first goals of the season."

"You're right," Keisha grunted, a smile playing shyly on her lips.

Cathy looked back and forth between the two of them. "They had us on the ropes, and you two just gave them a knockout punch." Olivia saw a twinkle grow in Cathy's eyes. "Kennedy-Owens. Keisha-Olivia. *KO*. Knockout."

Olivia saw grins spreading along the bench. Even Coach Hicks broke her poker face to crack a tiny smile. Olivia muttered, "I'm not sure about this."

"Me, either," Keisha echoed.

Hicks snickered. "What a shock. You two actually agree on something. Unfortunately for you both, this nickname is definitely going to be a thing. Now, put your focus back on the game. You're going out again."

Olivia's shoulders slumped.

Cathy leaned over to whisper, "Quit pouting. It's cute. Plus, we're the next shift."

The trio took the ice a minute later on a partial change. Cathy dumped the puck into the offensive zone for Olivia to chase down behind the net. She kicked the puck free to Keisha who fed Cathy for a perfect one-timer that clanged off the post. Keisha scooped up the rebound and passed it back to Olivia, who was denied at point blank range. Chicago's goalie covered up the puck before it escaped, and Olivia's line skated off after a brief scuffle with the frustrated Chicago defenders.

Misty fist bumped Olivia as they passed each other. "Good shift, bad bounces," the younger woman said. Bouchard slammed a goal home late in the second period to send the Blossoms to the locker room up by three.

"Settle down, people. Chicago is perfectly capable of scoring three goals in one period, so don't get cocky. Let's play our game, keep cool, and put this away."

On Olivia's first shift, they caught Chicago overextended again. Seeing her chance, she zipped a pass to Keisha, but Hazlett swatted it down. Chicago broke the other way, racing toward the Blossoms net. Olivia dove to cut off a centering pass but mistimed the dive and could only watch helplessly as the puck flew past her nose for an easy one timer goal.

Back on the bench, Keisha was furious. "What the hell kind of bullshit pass was that, bitch? Next time, lead me."

"Fuck you. If I led you any more, it would have been icing."

"Come on, y'all. Settle down." Cathy placed her hands, one on each shoulder. "Mistakes happen."

"Bullshit," Keisha growled.

"Yeah, like you never fuck up. Screw you, bitch."

"Both of you, stuff it," Hicks hissed. "Get your heads back in the game, or I will bench your line."

Olivia shut her mouth, grateful that Keisha did the same. Their next two shifts were uneventful. Olivia picked up another bruise blocking a shot, and Cathy clanged another shot off the post.

"I'm sorry. My shots just aren't going in today," Cathy said as they skated to the bench.

Olivia comforted the young winger. "Look at me. The post giveth, and the post taketh away. Next game those shots will go in. I promise."

Misty scored on an empty net for the Blossoms' fourth goal, and Olivia's line closed out the game, playing keep away for the final few seconds until the buzzer.

Svetlana, Keisha, and Olivia earned the three stars of the game, waving to the cheering fans before exiting the rink. Hicks congratulated the team on a job well done, rewarding them with a rare day off. "Enjoy it, because we're going on the road against Detroit, Pittsburgh, and Minnesota, then home and away against Vancouver before we close out the year in Toronto on New Year's Eve. That's going to be a circus."

Olivia was looking forward to the away game at Vancouver because she'd have a chance to see Maxim the night before. Then they'd see each other again in New York on Valentine's Day. She needed to keep his attention focused on the wedding.

As if she needed more of a reminder, her mother texted her that night. Not to congratulate her on her goal or the win, but to harangue her about Maxim, his continued indiscretions, and the upcoming wedding. *As if Maxim's inability to keep his dick in his pants is* my *fault. So long as he's disappointing a different woman every night, I'm okay.* Olivia checked social media again. The ignorant Russian's antics were a constant source of humiliation, but once they were married, she would at least get her parents off her back. *Of course, our forced separation helped me realize how much I don't want him in bed with me every night. At least here I can satisfy myself with my toys without hurting his fragile male ego.*

Olivia pulled out her trusty magic wand and slid off her underwear. She smiled as the sound of her vibrator filled the air. Olivia moaned as she pressed it to her clitoris.

Chapter 10

If You Want Blood, You've Got It
AC/DC

Keisha moaned as Kelly's tongue circled her clitoris. *Or is it Shelly? Fuck, I can't remember. I'll just try not to mention a name, and hope she doesn't notice.* She ran her fingers through Kelly/Shelly's blue hair, gripping to show her appreciation for the sensations on her clit. *Damn, I love pulling on this woman's hair. So soft and silky. I like her tattoos, too. Maybe I will celebrate my contract with some fresh ink.* Keisha groaned as Kelly/Shelly eagerly lapped her drenched pussy.

This was her fourth different bedmate on four consecutive nights. At least this one had heard of hockey before. Not that she minded spreading hockey knowledge around. She didn't mind spreading her legs, either, especially when her companion was as eager as this one. *I really need to learn her name, because she's worthy of a repeat performance. Oh, damn. Whatever she's doing with her fingers right now, I need to learn it. Holy shit.*

Keisha looked down to see blue eyes looking back, dancing with delight as the other woman elicited moan after groan. She threw her head back as she fell apart, convulsing and whimpering. Satiated, Keisha pulled her up for a sensuous kiss. "Whatever you just did, teach me so I can return the favor."

"Sure thing, umm..."

She giggled. "It's Keisha. Don't feel bad, because I can't remember, is your name Kelly or Shelly?"

"Shelly. Now I don't feel like a complete idiot about forgetting your name."

"Same. Now let me make you feel good, Shelly."

They exchanged numbers in the morning, and Keisha promised to text once the Blossoms were back in Portland. Neither of them were looking for a relationship, but Keisha wasn't going to turn down the chance for more good sex. *Plus, I'll have a chance to pack more clothes when we're in Minneapolis.*

Keisha watched videos of Detroit and Pittsburgh as the team waited at PDX for their flight. Hicks wandered over and sat down. Keisha glanced at her coach, who leaned closer to the screen.

"What are you looking for?"

"Flaws. Patterns. Everyone has habits. It's just a matter of what is exploitable."

Hicks nodded. "Which is exactly what I do. I'm curious how you see these weaknesses."

"Honestly, it's something I picked up in college. I wasn't really allowed to coach, so I focused on player development. I looked for habits our players developed which other teams could exploit and came up with ways to adjust. Everyone has habits and tendencies, and generally, they aren't bad, but they can sometimes still be exploited. Once I started noticing people's tendencies, it became my thing."

Hicks swapped seat assignments to put Keisha with the coaching staff for the flight. Keisha felt guilty about the change because she didn't feel like she found anything momentous about either Detroit or Pittsburgh. She also worried about getting a reputation for being the coach's favorite. When she brought up her concerns with Hicks, her coach snickered. "Owens, it's well known that I treat my favorites worse than everyone else."

"Not what I wanted to hear, either."

"Relax. You're smart, and I'm going to pick your brain relentlessly, but I'm also fair. I told Caine to lock you down ASAP. And, if you're interested in coaching as a career later on, then I'll provide whatever resources or mentoring I can."

"Thanks, coach."

"Don't thank me. You're getting extra hours in the film room for this."

Keisha smiled. It felt good to be seen and valued, especially since now she'd benefit from what she already did by habit.

She was assigned Cathy as her roommate for the trip. The pink-haired chatterbox proved to be a good companion. Cathy knew a great pizza place in Detroit from a visit during her college days, so they had an excellent meal together while most of the team suffered through typical American chain restaurant fare. After a nail-biting 3-2 overtime win in the Motor City, the Blossoms were off to Pittsburgh.

Keisha sat next to Cathy on the bus ride from the airport to the hotel, both of them gawking at the city as they rolled by. Cathy scrolled through her phone, providing Keisha with a running history of Pittsburgh. Keisha reveled in her young companion's enthusiasm.

Hicks gave the team the address of a local gym for team weight lifting before dinner. Cathy and Keisha changed and walked over to the gym. After draining her water bottle, Keisha went to refill it. She heard a voice around the corner and poked her head around to see Olivia muttering to herself while texting.

"Bitch, you're supposed to be working out, or are you too good for the rest of us?"

"Mind your own business," Olivia shot back.

"I'm stuck on a line with you until the coach decides otherwise, so your business is my business."

"No. It's not. Just leave me alone."

"Aw... Boy troubles? Did your Russian boytoy find someone better?"

"Fuck you." Olivia clenched her hands around her phone.

Keisha felt a rush of wicked pleasure upon seeing her rival's discomfort. "At least he didn't have to look hard to find your replacement. Any skank is an improvement over you."

Olivia growled and swung a fist. Keisha dodged backward, taking a grazing blow on her arm.

"Now it's on. Come on, Princess. What ya got?" Keisha backed up a bit, beckoning Olivia forward. The other woman charged forward, swinging wildly. Keisha ducked and punched Olivia in the gut. Olivia swung a knee up, and Keisha caught it awkwardly. This exposed her back and Olivia rained punches on her kidneys. Keisha lifted Olivia's leg and they toppled over together. The pair grunted and screamed as they writhed on the ground, punching whenever they had enough room to swing.

Keisha felt strong hands pulling her away. She saw Olivia being similarly restrained. They both thrashed against their captors, desperate to re-engage. Dani and Heike manhandled Keisha away, pulling her into the gym's locker room.

"What the hell, Keisha?" Heike snapped. "Just because Hicks is loving you these days doesn't mean you can get into fights."

"She threw the first punch," Keisha grumped, touching her face.

Dani spat, "What is this? Third grade? Tell me you didn't do anything to provoke her."

"I..." Keisha swallowed the lie and opted for truth instead. "She was on her phone instead of working out."

"Oh, and her looking at her screen is a good reason to fight?"

"Well..." Keisha knew she didn't have an answer.

Dani's furrowed eyebrows shadowed seething black eyes as her fingertip poked roughly into Keisha's sternum. "Save it. Get yourself cleaned up, then we're going to babysit you until we're done here.

You and Olivia obviously can't be trusted to keep your shit together off the ice."

Heike added, "Yeah. How is it you two can play beautifully together—and I do mean beautifully—yet off the ice, you hate each other?"

Keisha shrugged. "I don't know. Out there, it's different. Once we go over the boards, hockey is the only thing that matters. Back on the bench, she's the crazy bitch who broke my body because she's a sore fucking loser."

Dani and Heike looked at each other but said nothing.

"What? No words of wisdom or deep insight?" Keisha challenged her friends.

The big German shrugged her shoulders. "*Nein.*"

"Nada."

"Fine. Babysit me so we can get this over with." There were no further incidents while weight lifting or at dinner. Keisha could see Hicks and LeBeau talking during the meal, not even bothering to conceal their glances at her and Olivia. LeBeau came over to sit with Keisha. The French Canadian was a surefire hall-of-famer and a legend of the game. She was also team captain, sliding effortlessly into her mentor role when she took a seat.

"We need to speak about you and Kennedy."

"Look, I'm sorry about the fight earlier."

Sophie arched an eyebrow. "Are you?"

Keisha withered under the captain's glare. "Not really."

"You see? This is a problem."

"It's our problem, not yours."

"No, Owens. It's a *team* problem, which makes it *my* problem." She held up a slightly bent finger to forestall any reaction. "Do you have any idea how much I loathe mothering grown women? You're both old enough to do better. Yes, I realize there's bad blood. I watched the video. The three game suspension was bullshit for what she did to you. Hell, a year wouldn't have been enough."

"Why are we talking, then? Let me get mine back."

Sophie's lips turned down into a frown. "Blood doesn't make this right. Have you considered therapy?"

"*Therapy?* Are you fucking kidding me?"

Heads snapped around to look at them.

Keisha continued in a softer voice, "Olivia is the one who needs therapy, not me."

"Yes, therapy. You experienced serious trauma, and that leaves scars. Both on your skin and up here." Sophie tapped her head. "Seeking help to process your trauma isn't weak. Sometimes, opening up is the strongest thing you can do."

"I haven't considered it before, but you make a persuasive argument," Keisha muttered grudgingly.

"Please do. Coach is pissed with both of you." The captain held up her hand when Keisha opened her mouth. "You are, as you Americans say, a grown-ass woman. Act like it. I don't care how much you hate Kennedy. Coach doesn't tolerate immature behavior, and neither do I."

"Yes, Cap. It won't happen again."

"Good. Now, I'm going to go have the same damn talk with the Puck Princess."

Keisha felt like sulking in a corner. She left the table, returning to her room. Keisha threw herself in her bed, pulling the sheets around herself. When Cathy came back later, Keisha pretended to be asleep. This was its own special form of torture because she had to listen to her bubbly roommate get ready for bed with effervescent cheer.

Her mood was still sour through gameday practice. Dani and Heike tried to cheer her up, to no avail. Keisha felt better once she began pre-game warm-ups. Being on the ice helped submerge the turmoil in her mind. Once the puck dropped, Keisha felt focused and energized.

Jensen forced the Pittsburgh goalie to cover up for an offensive zone face-off. The second line stood for a shift change when Hicks snapped, "Kennedy, Owens, Miller. Get out there." Keisha shook her head in surprise, but stood and skated out onto the ice. She could hear surprised muttering from the bench but put it out of her mind.

Keisha parked herself on the left edge of the face-off circle, facing Pittsburgh's right wing and their goalie. She kept her eye on the puck as the official held it above the dot. Olivia won it cleanly on the draw, slipping the puck between her legs where Dani collected it at the blue line.

Meanwhile, Keisha surged forward, planting herself in front of the crease. Dani whipped a low wrist shot toward the net. Keisha brought her stick down to meet the puck in the air, tipping it upwards. The rubber disc fluttered past the goalie's glove and into the goal.

There was a moment of stunned silence in the arena before the air was filled with loud booing. She felt a stick hammer into her back, courtesy of Pittsburgh's infuriated right wing. Keisha turned directly into a punch that rattled her helmet cage. Before she could recover, a pink and white blur interposed itself between Keisha and the next punch. She felt arms pulling her from the melée as black-and-gold battled white-and-pink in front of the net. Keisha quickly looked at the faces around her. *Cathy, Dani, and Heike... Which only leaves...* Gloves dropped and fists swung and a turn of the combatants revealed a blonde mane peeking out from below the helmet above a Blossom jersey with the number ninety-eight on prominent display as Olivia connected a wild roundhouse punch to the chest of the Pittsburgh player. Referees managed to separate the scrum. After the referees deliberated on the severity of the penalties, Olivia earned a two minute minor penalty, while the Pittsburgh winger was in the box for four minutes on a double minor.

Misty scored during the four-on-four play, then Olivia added a power play goal after she exited the penalty box, giving the Blossoms a three goal lead before the first period was halfway done. Olivia fist bumped the team along the bench before sitting down with them.

Keisha hissed, "What the hell was that?"

Olivia swiveled her head to stare at Keisha. "Don't read anything into it. I needed to hit someone, and Cap says I'm not allowed to hit you."

A few players down the bench, Sophie snorted. "At least one of you two listened to me."

"Good, because I can fight my own battles. Don't think this clears any of the debt you owe me." Keisha was seething inside, clenching and unclenching her fists reflexively.

"Go fuck yourself, Keisha. It's not always about you."

"Oh, trust me, I know, Princess. It's always about you."

Cathy, looking miserable between them, had evidently had enough. "Shut up, shut up, shut up," she exclaimed. "You're both horrible, and you drag everyone down. *Just. Please. Stop.*"

Keisha looked down at her hands, unable to meet Cathy's gaze. The pink-haired pixie was probably the kindest person Keisha had ever met, and she felt awful for upsetting her. "I'm sorry," Keisha mumbled, echoed by Olivia.

They sat in forlorn silence until Hicks asked, "Are you all done with your bullshit drama, or should I send out the second line?"

All three answered with some form of, "Ready, coach."

"Great. You're the next shift. Get your damned heads in the game, and don't make me regret this."

Keisha netted her second goal late in the third period on a perfect pass from Olivia. She felt a giddy rush watching the crowd slowly stream out after her goal. Her gleeful feeling persisted into the locker room as the Blossoms recorded their first-ever shutout.

Back in the hotel room, Keisha hugged Cathy. "I'm sorry again about earlier."

Cathy nodded and squeezed her tight. "Are you sorry enough to do something about it? I understand your history with Olivia, but this toxicity isn't good for you, either. You need something more in your heart than hate."

"Maybe there's love in there, too."

The younger woman snorted against her chest. "If there were, you would have talked about it."

Keisha considered her expansive history of failed relationships and one-night stands, predominantly the latter lately. Lots of lust, not much love. Keisha's chest heaved. "You're right about the lack of love." She grinned, attempting to steer the conversation in a light-hearted direction. "Any chance you're interested?"

Cathy snorted again. "Sadly, I'm not gay. Otherwise, I totally would."

"If you change your mind…"

Unsurprisingly, Cathy didn't change her mind by the time their plane touched down in Minneapolis, but she was a pleasant seat-mate all the same. Keisha squealed in delight when the team exited the terminal. She raced forward to embrace her mother, followed by her friend Sharon. Sharon's daughter Liza was brimming with questions about being a professional hockey player. Before she could answer the young girl's questions, Keisha endured Tamika Owens' interrogation about life in Portland and with the Blossoms. The unspoken subject of many of Tamika's queries walked out of the terminal, tracked by angry eyes. Keisha noted how no family greeted Olivia, and she instead trudged directly onto the team bus.

Tamika growled, "How do you play next to that"—she caught herself before using a rare expletive, realizing Liza was present—"woman?"

"It's a struggle, Mama. But it's worth it to live my dream."

"You're playing so well, baby. I can't imagine where you'd be if she hadn't taken so much from you."

"I know." Keisha gripped her mother's arm. "Didn't you always tell me that the past is the past? Nothing we do changes it. We just have to move forward?"

"Yeah." Her mother smiled and cupped Keisha's cheek like she'd done since she was a child. "Saying it doesn't always make it easy."

"Truth."

The Blossoms left Minneapolis with one point gained in the standings from an overtime loss. Keisha met up with Chuck and the rest of the Vipers after the game. She missed her old team, but their encouragement of her newfound success at the professional level warmed her heart. Meanwhile, Keisha left Minneapolis with more clothes and a new contract through the end of the next season. Secured of staying in Portland for at least another year and a half, she resigned from her current job and began searching for a volunteer gig in Portland.

At least professional hockey pays enough to live on. I liked my old job, though, and hopefully I can find a way to use my skills and help people in Portland. Too many people in this country live paycheck-to-paycheck and it's fucking stressful. Speaking of stress, I should see if Shelly is free tonight for some breast and relaxation.

Chapter 11

Pink Pony Club

Chappell Roan

Olivia looked at the check from her most recent modeling gig and did the math. She wasn't going to have enough money to cover rent and still eat. One other option was to cut back on clothes, styling, and make-up. Another was to find a job that would pay enough to cover rent in less than two weeks.

I'm already living in a dump. I need food to live. I also need to maintain my social media presence so my stupid fucking fiancé doesn't forget my existence, which requires money. My parents don't have money anymore, which is why I'm marrying a complete moron whose father is probably neck deep with the Russian mob. I've spent my entire life chasing my parents' expectations, especially after they kicked Pat out, and yet they can't even bother to acknowledge my recent successes.

Every conversation is about Maxim, and how I'm not doing enough for the wedding.

I can't afford to be homeless. Eating is essential. I have to maintain my image for my parents' well-being. Thus, I need a second job that pays enough money to make rent. Olivia stared at the new dress hanging on the garment rack. *Buying something new every time I feel bad isn't helping. Which makes me feel bad. Which makes me want to buy something. I can't buy anything, because my credit cards are maxed out and rent is due. Which is why I need another job. Or sex work. I need money fast. Fuck.*

Olivia contacted a friend from college who she knew stripped back in college. They'd kept in touch off and on. Her friend had transitioned to online only during the pandemic and promised to ask around. Meanwhile, Olivia did her own research and found a local strip club which sometimes allowed dancers to go on stage right after an audition. After the team returned from Minneapolis, she put on a substantial amount of make-up and a hot pink wig and went to the club.

She auditioned for the manager, silently grateful that she was only required to strip naked and not perform anything extra. Her moves were a bit rusty as she hadn't stripped since a wild Spring Break in Cancun during college, but Olivia was athletic and creative enough to get hired. The manager wasn't thrilled about her limited availability, especially since she was deliberately vague about her real job, but he had plenty of girls willing to work more shifts, so Olivia ended up with the dregs of the schedule.

Olivia collected a measly wad of dollars on her first appearance on stage. She bit back her disappointment when she only added a few more bills on her next trip. Her mind raced, trying to decide if stripping would be enough to get rent paid. Olivia's third time on stage was going slightly better when she noted two women playing tonsil hockey. They broke apart, and the one with blue hair waved a twenty near the edge of the stage. Olivia strutted over to dance in front of them. She bent over, fully exposing herself and leering at the blue-haired woman when the woman's dark-skinned companion leaned forward into the light. Olivia felt the icy grip of terror grasp her heart as she recognized Keisha.

Whipping her head up, Olivia almost fled the stage, but the rational part of her brain kicked in, reminding her of just how desperately she needed the twenty dollar bill dangling in the patron's hand. Blue beckoned her, and Olivia reluctantly squatted down, her guts recoiling at the thought of being fully exposed in front of Keisha. Apparently the make-up, pink wig, and lighting disguised her appearance enough, because she saw no hint of recognition on her rival's face. She did see a second twenty subtly slide next to the first. Blue whispered, "It's all yours if you kiss me, and you'll get another if you kiss my friend."

I don't want to kiss another woman, and I really *don't want to kiss Keisha, but I need the money.* Olivia prayed she would remain anonymous as she leaned forward to kiss the blue-haired woman. The crowd cheered wildly, filling Olivia's veins with bounteous bravado. She kissed Keisha, eye-to-eye with the woman who would cheerfully punch her. There was still no glimmer of recognition.

Collecting the three twenties and a small cloud of cash as her set ended, Olivia slipped backstage.

"What the hell were you thinking out there?" The manager hissed.

"Guys love some girl-on-girl action. The crowd ate it up." Olivia tried to act nonchalant, even as her heart pounded like a drum solo. The manager grunted, but provided no further comment.

By the end of the night, after the cut for the club, plus tips for the bouncers, the bartenders, and the DJ, Olivia walked out with just under two hundred dollars. *This gets me about half of what I need. Given my other shifts, I'll probably barely squeak by this month. No more shopping, though.*

Keisha gave no indication that she recognized Olivia at practice the next day. Their home and away series with Vancouver was fast approaching, along with her opportunity to see Maxim, as his team would be in Vancouver for an away game scheduled the night after Olivia's. Two games and the daily grind of practices helped keep her mind off the nagging worries about paying bills, at least until she was stuck alone on Christmas. She was able to pick up a shift at the strip club, which wasn't terribly lucrative and mostly made her feel even more miserable, but she had enough money for rent, food, and the bare minimum for her credit card bills.

Olivia's spirits fell further when her friend got back to her about a paying opportunity in Vegas. After expenses, it would net Olivia about a thousand dollars—she would just need to have sex with two men on camera. She reached out to the performers to work on details, assuring herself that she could back out at any time. Her friend walked her through the process of setting up her own fans site along with a list of equipment to purchase to make money from online sex work. She contacted a local Portland group which assisted people with overcoming an addiction to shopping and asked for help.

The prospect of starting *another* form of sex work to pay the bills consumed Olivia's thoughts, leading to a mild reprimand from Hicks to pay attention.

"Liv, get your head in the game," Cathy spat. "We're the next shift."

Shaking her head, Olivia refocused on the still scoreless game. The Blossoms fans were rocking the coliseum, excited their team was showing signs of life after a dismal start. Bouchard dumped the puck, heading for the bench as Olivia and her line lifted themselves onto the boards.

As each member of the second line came off, the third line skaters dropped to the ice. Vancouver passed the puck forward, and Keisha clobbered their right wing just as she received the puck. Olivia pounced on the bouncing disk, corralling it with her stick as she crossed the blue line. The goalie had her square on, and the back defender sprawled on the ice, cutting off the passing lane to Cathy. Olivia swung behind the net, looking for a wraparound goal, but the goalie was already lined up on the post. Her head came up in time to see Keisha charging the slot, and Olivia whipped the puck in front of the crease, right onto the tape of Keisha's stick who buried it in the back of the net. Sirens blared, and the crowd went ballistic as the Blossoms celebrated.

They hung on for a one-zero victory which left Olivia emotionally and physically drained. She still felt exhausted as the team climbed aboard a plane for the short flight north into British Columbia. Olivia wanted to nap, but sleep eluded her racing mind. She decided to see how her time with Maxim went before choosing whether she would take the Vegas gig. She texted Maxim the moment she could, elated he was already in Vancouver. Not long after the team bus arrived at the hotel, she was in his room.

"Oh, Maxim. You're so big. And so good. I've missed you so much." The lies were well-practiced and effortless by now. Olivia rolled her hips with feigned enthusiasm to meet Maxim's uninspiring thrusts.

"Why I must wear condom?"

He asks the same stupid question every time. It gets more annoying each time he asks. I'd rather not have sex with him at all.

"Because we don't want a surprise for the wedding, my love." Olivia rolled her eyes in frustration—her exasperation only increased by knowing Maxim probably thought the gesture meant he was a sex god.

Also, because I tasted some other woman's pussy on your dick, you fucking idiot. I'm not getting some disease because of your stupidity. The Vegas gig is happening. Hopefully at least one of those guys knows how to please a woman.

"Wedding, right. Urgh," he grunted. "When is wedding?"

"Next summer. You make me feel so good. I'm really looking forward to our honeymoon." Olivia couldn't think of anything worse than a week of awful sex with Maxim.

"Urgh," he grunted again as his face contorted into an expression he seemed to consider especially virile. "I'm..."

"Oh yes, give it to me," Olivia squealed, faking an orgasm. She felt a rush of relief when he rolled off of her. "We should talk about the wedding. Your father submitted a guest list to the wedding planner, but don't you want some of your teammates there?"

"*Da.* You should invite them."

Olivia repressed a scream of frustration. "They're your teammates, my love," she choked out. "You also need to approve the wedding colors. Then we'll need to decide between a band or a deejay, and—" Any further discussion was curtailed by a bear-like snore. Olivia's fingernails bit into her palms, and she threw her head back in defeat. It was all she could do not to beat her hands into the mattress—or more satisfyingly, her fiancé's cretinous skull. A thunderous and revolting fart sent her fleeing across the room. Olivia held her nose against the vile vapors as she collected her clothes.

She found sanctuary in the hotel gym, partially working out her frustrations on the cold iron. Her focus didn't crack when Keisha and Cathy joined her in the gym. Olivia kept her headphones in, ignoring her foe's presence.

Olivia didn't even crack a smile when Hicks announced prior to the game that the third line was tasked with defending against Vancouver's top line. Cathy nudged her. "What is with you, Liv?"

"Sorry. I've got a lot on my mind."

"Oh, you saw Maxim, didn't you? Did you talk about wedding stuff?"

Not wanting to get into the details, Olivia shaded her words. "Yeah. Wedding. Life. Just a lot going on right now."

Her friend smiled. "Tell me if you need anything, even if it's just to talk."

Olivia nodded. "Thanks, Cat. Your support means a lot."

Cathy's face lit up as she squealed. "You gave me a nickname. Now I know we're friends." Olivia reached over to squeeze Cathy's hand as the team stood up to march to the ice.

Not that I can talk to her about what's going on. I'm living so many lies I can barely keep track of them all, and in a few days I'm flying to Vegas to fuck two men I've never met so I can finance this house of cards. I need a friend more than anything right now, but I can't let her or anyone see behind the farcical façade of my life.

Skating out into the faceoff circle at center ice didn't bring her calm, but it helped focus her problems down to one small black disc. Olivia bent down, her stick vibrating with anticipation as she awaited the puck drop. The two centers scrabbled for control, skates and sticks battering the black rubber until her opponent finally kicked it out. Cathy pounced on the loose puck, beginning her own battle for control. After a brief spat, she sent it sailing into the offensive zone where Keisha chased it into a corner, stick slapping against the boards as a defender crashed into her.

Shift after shift, Olivia's line waged a grueling campaign against Vancouver's best. Her body felt like a series of bruises and welts from body checks and blocked shots. It was glorious.

The score was tied at one after three periods. Hicks called out, "Kennedy, Owens, Cruz. You're the first shift in overtime." Olivia experienced a rush of adrenaline and pride. Three on three hockey left a lot of open ice, and this was her moment to shine. She won the faceoff back to Daniella, who skated carefully forward, reading Vancouver's movements. Daniella whipped a pass to Keisha, who carried the puck across the blue line before sliding it back to Daniella. Olivia circled to the right as Keisha crashed the net. Keisha camped out in front of the goalie as Olivia raced across the slot. In the corner of her eye, Olivia caught Daniella moving in the opposite direction. Her charge brought the goalie to the left side of the net, Keisha shadowed along to restrict the goalie's view. Olivia flicked the puck behind her, and Daniella whipped a one time shot that clanged off the post, ricocheted off the goalie's back, and dribbled across the line for the game-winning goal.

The three of them converged, celebrating as the crowd rained down boos. Daniella cackled, "Great pass and an ugly goal. But ugly still counts."

"Yes, it does," Olivia crowed right before the rest of the team mobbed them excitedly. *As ugly as my life is right now, I hope it's all worth it.*

Chapter 12

Turn The Page

Bob Seger and The Silver Bullet Band

The flight to Toronto was a nightmare. The plane dodged storms all the way across the Great Plains, bouncing and jostling the passengers. Keisha did her best to tune out the flight and focus on watching tape, but her efforts came to naught once Heike blew chunks into an air sickness bag. The smell induced Dani to throw up, and suddenly the stench of vomit permeated the cabin. Fighting down her queasy stomach, Keisha retreated into meditation.

Groans filled the cabin when the pilot announced that the plane was landing in Detroit. The team filed off the plane in Detroit as Hicks yelled at Caine over the phone. A bus was arranged to drive the team to Toronto. Normally around a five hour drive, the snowy conditions threatened to extend the team's adversity well into the night.

They had just crossed the border into Windsor when the bus' heater broke down. Sophie LeBeau's head rested on her shoulder, the captain snoring peacefully in Keisha's ear as Keisha stared out the window at the snow falling in the night. Glancing over Sophie's head, she regarded her two linemates across the aisle. Olivia had her arm around Cathy, whose teeth were visibly chattering. Keisha observed Olivia shimmying off her coat to wrap around the two of them. Dani and Heike were squashed together in the seat in front of Cathy and Olivia, also huddling for warmth.

Keisha snuggled closer to Sophie as the temperature continued to drop. The two of them pulled off their coats to turn into makeshift blankets containing their combined body heat.

A midnight stop at Tim Hortons was met with jubilation as the team flooded into the indoor warmth. They collectively stocked up on glazed carbs and hot beverages, walking around to push blood into their aching toes. Filing back out into the frigid white night, the team grabbed their bags from under the bus. As the vehicle lumbered back on the highway, the players and coaches submerged under piles of clothing, huddling with each other for warmth.

Keisha tried to ignore the scent of Sophie filling her nostrils. Rumor had it that Sophie's marriage was on the rocks, but Keisha knew better than to try anything, especially with her captain. She regretted not seeing Shelly last night. *I was supposed to be in Toronto, finding a hook-up right now, not drowning in the scent of an untouchable woman.*

Sleep eventually caught up with her, dragging her into uncomfortable dreams. Keisha woke to the sound of snow crunching under tires. She opened a bleary eye to see a bright outline of a sign through frost-encrusted windows. "Tim Hortons again?"

"Yeah," Hicks answered, leaning on the seats on either side of the aisle. Raising her voice, she bellowed, "Rise and shine. We're one to two hours from the hotel, depending on road conditions. There's bathrooms, coffee, and breakfast inside. The team is buying. Also, save your receipts from earlier, if you have them. I'm putting *every* expense I can on Caine's tab."

There were scattered cheers as heads popped out like prairie dogs from under piles of jerseys and jackets. Keisha could see Hicks counting heads as the team disembarked and raced inside the warm shop. "Thanks, coach," Keisha said as she passed.

Hicks' grin was fierce. "My pleasure, Owens."

They reached the hotel two hours later. Everyone stuffed their clothing haphazardly into bags as they stretched out the kinks in their backs. Hicks addressed the team, "I want everyone to hit the gym, the pool, or both today. Get your bodies moving. Otherwise, take the day off. We all deserve it after this mess." Cheers broke out. "Kennedy, Owens. See me inside."

In the lobby, Keisha found Olivia standing next to Hicks. The coach grinned before saying, "I've got bad news and good news for you two. Bad news, the media wants to talk to you. Good news, I convinced them to do separate sessions."

Curious, Keisha asked, "Why is the media bad news?"

Hicks snickered, "Wait until they start asking questions. You'll figure it out. Owens, you're on at three. Kennedy, you're on at four."

After a restful nap, Keisha got herself together for a briefing with the team's media representative just minutes before the press session. "You're probably going to get some stupid questions, and you'll almost certainly get some uncomfortable questions. Keep your cool, don't let them rattle you. 'No comment' is always an option. Oh, and you will probably get the same question multiple times. Just be cool and patient."

Keisha nodded. "Got it. Anything else?" she asked.

The media rep shot her a dirty look. "Yeah, I spent four years in college, then got myself a Master's, plus almost ten years of job experience. I've got tons more to tell you, but you get the thirty second version because that's all the time you gave me."

Keisha studied the carpet, too embarrassed to look at the woman. "I'm sorry."

She sighed. "It's fine. I'm sorry. I slept like shit, and it's been a long ass day. Go in there, find your happy place, and stay there. You'll do great."

There was a desk and a microphone set up for Keisha in front of a dozen journalists plus cameras. Keisha waved shyly as she sat down. "Hi, y'all."

"Patricia Robotaille, Hockey News Tonight. You've had a magical run through your first few games. What do you attribute your success to?"

Keisha took a deep breath. *Stay cool. Be nice. Find your happy place.* "Great question, Patricia. Being off the ice for so many years, teams don't have much tape on me. Yet." She grinned for the cameras.

"Heather LaFontaine, Canadian Broadcasting. Speaking of your many years off the ice, what's it like playing with Olivia Kennedy? The woman who almost disabled you."

Deep breath. You knew this was coming. "Thanks for the question, Heather. As you might imagine, there are some feelings there. Once we're out on the ice, the only thing that matters is playing the best we can for our team and our city."

"Mitch Carlson, Canadian Hockey Network. Rumor has it there have been multiple fistfights between you and Olivia Kennedy. Is that true?"

"Thank you, Mitch. I'm not going to dignify rumors."

"So, everything is fine?"

"We're not friends, if that's what you're asking. But like I said, we're professionals and we bring our best for our team and our city."

"Stephanie Griggs, Women's ESPN. How do you like Portland?"

"Thank you, Stephanie. Can I say how much it irritates me to have Women's ESPN? You're a journalist, I'm a hockey player. We both kick ass at what we do. I'm not just fluffing your ego. I've watched a ton of your reporting. You know a shitload more than most of the bobbleheads over on the ESPN which doesn't have a gender attached. Also, am I allowed to say shitloads?"

The collected journalists laughed, and Stephanie blushed.

"Sorry. Back to your original question. I love Portland. I miss Minneapolis, obviously. I grew up there, but Portland welcomed me with open arms. Next question."

Keisha forcefully backed Stephanie Griggs into the wall, kissing her with wild abandon. They'd run into each other in the hotel lobby that evening and Stephanie took Keisha out for dinner, expensed to the network. Returning to Stephanie's hotel room, their tongues and fingers busily explored every open patch of skin they could find. They tugged frantically at each other's clothing to expose more explorable skin as they stumbled toward the bed.

"I really shouldn't do this."

Keisha lifted her head away from Stephanie's neck. "Me either, but damn, you taste good." She snaked back down to run her tongue from Stephanie's collarbone to her jawline, then up to her ear. "Do you have any idea how many nights I got myself off after watching you?" Keisha growled lustfully.

Stephanie moaned, her fingernails scraping Keisha's shirt up her back. "A lot?"

"Almost every fucking night."

"Oh, God. Don't stop," Stephanie croaked. "This is okay, then, right? Wish fulfillment."

Keisha hummed deep in her throat as she gnawed on Stephanie's ear. Hearing the other woman whimper as her back arched sent a thrill of pleasure directly to Keisha's aching clit. They stopped long enough to yank off the rest of their clothes before they dove back into each other's lips. Keisha dug two fingers deep into Stephanie's lush garden, tantalizing her g-spot while Keisha's thumb worked her bud.

Stephanie latched on to Keisha's head with both hands, pulling her into a deep kiss. Keisha felt Stephanie's manicured fingers tracing the lines of her undercut before diving into the thick curls on top of her head.

"Is it okay that I touched your hair? I've never, you know…"

"Been with a Black woman before?"

The blonde woman nodded.

"Yeah. Just don't say weird shit about my hair. Actually, let me put your lips back to better use." Keisha shoved her tongue deep inside the other woman's mouth, savoring her groans as Keisha's fingers worked her toward a climax.

As Stephanie lay panting, Keisha brought one drenched finger up to her own mouth, then proffered the other finger to Stephanie, who gasped, "kinky," before she eagerly slurped her own juices. Once Stephanie recovered, she slid down Keisha's body and began lapping her pussy eagerly. Keisha ran her hands through the blonde's hair, encouraging her earnest efforts.

Keisha didn't mean to fall asleep in Stephanie's bed; however, mutual exhaustion won out. She was thankful no one witnessed her walk of shame, not that Keisha felt shameful at all, at least until she reached her room.

Cathy gave her a baleful eye, noting her wrinkled attire. "Where were you? I was worried when you didn't tell me you'd be out."

"I'm sorry. I just got caught up with...something."

The pink-haired woman snickered. "You mean someone."

"Okay, yeah."

Cathy's lips turned down into a worried frown. "I don't mean to slut shame you or anything, but is this normal for you? Don't you want to find someone more permanent?"

Keisha felt momentarily defensive before calming down. "Normally, I'd rip someone's head off for asking such a personal question, but I know you're just concerned."

"I'm not just concerned, Keisha. I'm your friend. If sleeping with a different woman each night is what works for you, then of course I'll support you..."

"Aw. You're sweet, thank you. I sense a 'but' coming, though."

The smaller woman stood up and embraced Keisha. "Oof." Cathy wrinkled her nose. "You smell like sex. Anyway, like I was saying, I'll support you, but I'm sensing that this sexual smorgasbord isn't what makes you happy. I want you to be happy."

"Sorry about the smell. Let me take a shower first, okay?"

The warm water helped Keisha contemplate what to say. *I wasn't aware Cathy considered me a friend. It's nice to have one, especially since everyone I know is so far away. She asks a good question. Am I happy? I'm having some great sex—which is good—but not with anyone I care about. A girlfriend would be nice. Maybe there's a cute girl at the new volunteer gig, or at least someone with a cute friend. It's been a while since I had someone permanent in my life.*

"Okay. We can talk now," Keisha said as she exited the bathroom.

"*Yay.*" Cathy clapped her hands together. "Thank you, Key." She paused, her face scrunching up in distaste. "Nope. Now that I said it, it sounds wrong."

Keisha roared with laughter at her friend's nickname attempt. Wiping her eyes, Keisha responded, "Yeah, I would have vetoed Key. Same with Kay."

Cathy looked disappointed. "I know it's stupid, but I like to have nicknames for my friends."

"It's not stupid...Cat." Keisha couldn't help but grin in response to the look of delight on Cathy's face at the nickname. "We'll come up with something, okay?"

"Thank you. Can I hug you again?"

"Sure. Oof." Keisha grunted at Cathy's enthusiastic embrace. "And thank you for caring about my happiness. I'm not usually like this. I'm stressed about moving to a new city, playing professional hockey, and being around"—Keisha remembered in time that Cathy and Olivia were also friends and searched for a different term—"someone who caused me so much pain. Yes, I'd much rather have a steady girlfriend, but finding one takes time and stability. So yeah, I guess I've been trying to fill the void with random sex."

Cathy tittered as she sat back down on her bed. "You said 'fill the void.'"

Keisha threw a sock at her. "You have a dirty mind."

"Says the woman who came back smelling like pussy," she retorted as she volleyed the sock back.

"Wait. Didn't you say you were straight?"

Cathy looked downward shyly. "I've smelled myself."

"Uh-huh."

She continued softly, "And I had a threesome once."

Keisha leaned forward. "Oh, really?"

"It was a one-time thing. A birthday present for my best friend in college. I mean…it was okay, but not my thing."

"There's nothing wrong with figuring out what works for you. Thank you for telling me, Cat. You're very brave."

"Really?"

"Yes. Really. You're the kindest person I know, and I'm sorry you're always caught between the shit with me and Olivia. It's not fair to you." Cathy shot up from her bed and wrapped her arms around Keisha again. She could feel the smaller woman's body shudder as Cathy started crying. Keisha held her tight, rubbing her back soothingly.

"I love you both." Cathy choked out a laugh between the tears. "I mean, not like sexy love, you know. You're both my friends, and I know there's history between you. I might not be able to change the past, but I know neither of you are happy, and I want to help."

"You do help," Keisha assured her.

Before the game that night, Keisha walked up to Olivia at her cubby. "Let's get Cathy some points tonight. She deserves it for putting up with us."

Olivia nodded. "Good call. I like it."

Chapter 13

Roxanne

The Police

Olivia nodded. "Good call. I like it." She looked over at Anton, the man she was about to have sex with, as they each reviewed their list of do's-and-don't's.

"Same. So what's our plan?"

"I'm thinking we start with kissing against the wall, like we're coming back from a date. Then, I'll partially strip you and blow you. After you cum, you go down on me. From there, maybe cowgirl, pretzel dip, doggy, then finally missionary before you pull out and cum on my tits."

"Cool. Let's map it out to make sure the cameras are in the right spots."

"Sounds good. About the blow job. Do you have enough in the tank to cum twice, or should I stop before you pop?"

"I can go for two. Should I get you off when I go down?"

"Yes, please. Only seems fair."

"Got it."

I can't believe this is what my life has come to. Between stripping, my online sex work—masturbation videos and now actual fucking porn, and hockey, I'm finally making enough money to pay rent, buy groceries, pay off a bit of my credit card bills, and keep up my bullshit social media image, so long as I keep my shopping under control. The irony of fucking some guy for my online content so I can afford to maintain a glamorous image to hold my fiancé's attention isn't lost on me.

I've screwed eight guys in the last five weeks. Anton will be number nine. I'm thankful for the International Break to have the extra time to make content. I should be able to pace releasing this content out over the next few months to keep building my brand.

With any luck, I can quit stripping after this week. Every time I'm up on stage, I'm terrified someone will see through my makeup and wig and recognize me. I still get shivers thinking about how dangerous it was to kiss Keisha and her girlfriend. Who knows what that bitch would have done if she'd recognized me.

Anton bent over to fiddle with the camera equipment. After a quick and positive appraisal of his ass, Olivia rechecked her wig and mask to make certain they were secure. She fluffed her tits and smiled at him as he stood up.

"Are you ready for the camera check?" she asked.

This is all temporary until the wedding. After Maxim and I are married, my money troubles go away. My parents' money troubles go away. Great. I'm effectively selling myself to Maxim for a gigantic pile of rubles. Which makes me a whore. I guess it's not any different than fucking Anton for money, either.

Unlike Maxim, I might actually cum with Anton, provided he's any good with his mouth. Maybe I should keep making videos after I'm married. At least with these guys there's a chance I might enjoy at least some of the sex. Maxim's dick does nothing for me, and the selfish bastard is certainly never going to go down on me.

One thing's for sure, I'm keeping my toy collection. Men might get me off occasionally, but my dildos and vibrators do it for me every time. Yet another thing I'll have to hide from Maxim.

I hate my life so much. Maxim. My parents. Stripping. Porn. It's a gigantic fucking mess, and I'm completely miserable. Oh, and hockey starts again next week, so I'll be seeing more of my insufferable nemesis. Well, at least Cathy will be there. The one bright spot in my life.

They finished the camera check and started filming. Olivia was thankful that Anton was good enough to make her cum orally. She did her best to appear enthusiastic as she faked her other orgasms and as Anton shot ropes of slimy semen on her chest and face.

The two of them reviewed the footage together, making sure they had enough for a quality video. "Damn. This is making me hot. Want to get it on again, just for fun this time?" Anton offered.

"No, thank you. Let's keep this strictly business."

"Sure. No problem. I'd be happy to work with you again. You're hot and a great fuck. Hit me up any time you're in LA."

Olivia noted the lack of distinction between work or pleasure in the last sentence, but chose to ignore it. "Definitely."

She was back at practice two days later, rent paid and enough sub-scribers to stop stripping. Having a little bit of financial security helped keep her head clear as she skated through drills. Olivia caught up with Coach Hicks at the end of practice. "Hey, coach."

"What's up, Kennedy?"

"Any chance you'll be shaking up the lines since Bollard is back from her injury?"

Hicks snickered. "What, you don't want to share a line with Miller any more?"

"I love skating with Cat, and you know I'm not talking about her."

"Of course I know. Look. You and Owens are like gasoline and matches off the ice, but out there"—Hicks gestured at the rink—"it's fucking beautiful."

"I know, but—"

Hicks brought her hand up, palm toward Olivia. "You should be *thanking* me for putting Owens on your line. In fact, you should be down on your knees, *begging* me not to break up your line. Do you want to know why?"

Olivia opened her mouth, but Hicks continued uninterrupted, "Because you were terrible before she got here. No goals, one assist. Your plus minus ratio was in the shitter. You couldn't win a face-off to save your life. Honestly, more than everything else, you looked like you were finished with hockey. Whatever spark you had a decade ago was gone."

The criticism was withering, but undisputable. Olivia felt the rising tide of shame and couldn't bear to meet Hicks' gaze.

"Then Owens shows up. I don't know why, but the two of you *work* together. Watching you skate, pass, or shoot is different now. Your spark is back." Hicks paused, her expression fierce. "No, not a spark. *Fire.* You look like you're having *fun* for the first time in years. Honestly, if you keep this up, then you'll be back on the National team soon. Owens, too."

"You think so?"

Hicks snorted. "I'm not blowing sunshine up your ass, Kennedy. Coaches talk. Your name is suddenly coming up a lot. You had two chances at the Olympics and shat the bed each time. Honestly, a month ago, you were Chernobyl-level radioactive, but now maybe you'll get a third chance to get it right."

Olivia lifted her head, a smile gracing her lips. "Getting back to the Olympics would be amazing."

Hicks' expression shifted into a stern frown. "Yeah, it would be. But it's not certain. You need to play like you belong. Owens makes you better, so you're stuck with her."

"Yes, coach." This time, she didn't sound upset.

"I am shaking up the lines, though. When we face Ottawa, you, Owens, and Miller are starting as the first line." Hicks huffed. "Close your damn mouth before you catch flies. And if you so much as breathe a word of this before I tell the team, then you'll be back to fourth line."

"Of course, coach," Olivia uttered with barely restrained glee.

In the locker room a few minutes later, Cathy asked, "What's up with Coach? She didn't look happy."

"It's all good news, Cat. I promise."

"All right." Cathy patted Olivia's hand. "I worry about you. You look a bit better today, but you seem tired and anxious a lot. Please tell me if I can do anything, even if it's just listening."

Olivia's heart melted. "Thank you. You're very good to me. It's just some stuff, but I'm handling it."

"Can we go out for dinner sometime soon? Catch up on the past few weeks?"

"Dinner would be great. Thank you."

Cathy's mouth shaped itself into a large 'O.' "Not tomorrow, though. I have a hair appointment. Should I stay pink, or try something else? I was thinking maybe magenta or royal purple."

Olivia laughed at her partner's passion. "I'm used to you with the pink hair, but I bet you'd look fantastic with any color."

"Aw, thanks, Liv. You're not helping me decide, but I appreciate the compliment. Okay, I gotta run. See you tomorrow."

Hicks announced the lineups for the Ottawa game the next day. Cathy greeted the news with her trademark exuberance, while Keisha gave it a taciturn nod. Olivia cringed every time she was near Keisha off the ice, but she admitted to herself that Hicks was right about their chemistry in the game.

Her line gave Ottawa a chemistry lesson with a four goal night, one each for Cathy, Heike, Keisha, and Olivia. The coliseum was rocking all game long, growing more raucous with each goal. Olivia exulted in every clean and smooth pass, her soul suffused with delight. *This* was why she played hockey. Not for the goals, or the wins, but for the exquisite sense of belonging. Olivia found a purity of purpose with the puck. She was made for moments like this.

Olivia's euphoria faded as she exited the building. Reality was often colder and harder than the ice she skated on. Out here in the non-hockey world, she had a threesome video to post and a masturbation video to film. There were emails from the wedding planner to respond to, and a text from her mother, asking about a rumor that Maxim was seeing someone else.

Before Olivia collapsed into a seething morass of nerves, her phone rang. "*Pat.* How are you?"

Her brother cackled. "*Me?* How are you? I watched your game. Livvy, you were *Ah May Zing.* Simply incredible. Even Bruce was spellbound, and you *know* how much he hates hockey."

"Yeah, it was really good." Olivia tried to recreate her earlier exultation, but it lingered frustratingly out of reach.

"Livvy, what's wrong?" Pat went from ecstatic and breezy to concerned and fully invested in an instant. "You can tell me anything."

"I know." A sob welled in her throat, barely contained.

"Come on, Livvy. I'm your brother. I love you unconditionally."

"I know." The sob broke free, followed by another and another.

"Let your feelings flow. I'm here to listen."

"Pat. I'm fucking up. Everything is completely and totally *fucked.*"

"What is it?"

"Shit. Fucking shit. Mom and Dad are going to kill me for this. For everything."

"Okay, now you're worrying me."

"They're broke, Pat. Mom and Dad are dead fucking broke. So am I, really."

"How?"

"I don't know. Crypto. Gambling. Who the hell knows. In my case, a shopping addiction I'm working through with support groups. Anyway, they made a deal, Pat. With Maxim's dad. You know, the Russian oligarch who is probably up to his neck in the mob?"

"Oh, fuck, Livvy," Patrick uttered in a heavy whisper.

"They need money. He has fucktons of money, but he can't legally bring it into the U.S."

"But if you marry Maxim…"

"Yeah. So I'm engaged to this useless moron so Mom and Dad can help his dad launder money—"

"Livvy, they sold you to the Russian mob."

"No shit, Pat." Olivia sobbed again. "I'm sorry. I didn't mean to take my shit out on you."

"What about Maxim? Do you even like him?"

"He's pretty, but nothing between the ears and worthless between the sheets."

"Ugh. Dated a few of those," Pat said with disgust.

Olivia choked out a messy hybrid of a laugh and another blubbering sniffle. "Stop. It's not funny."

"I know, Livvy."

"It gets worse. I'm doing porn because I need the money to maintain this glamorous image so Maxim doesn't get bored and dump me."

Her brother didn't hide the shock in his voice. "You're doing porn?"

"Yeah, for like five weeks now."

"Damn, Livvy. Why didn't you ask me for money?"

"Because, Pat. Our family has shit on you for fifteen years."

"You're my sister, and I love you. I'd do anything to keep you from porn, unless of course, you like making porn, then I will totally support you. Hashtag liberation."

"I mean, the sex is better than Maxim, but almost anything is. Still mostly disappointing, actually."

"But are they...you know..."

"What?"

"How are their trouser snakes? Are we talking garter snakes? Pythons? *Anacondas?*"

"You did not just ask me about the cocks of the guys I'm fucking to pay rent." Olivia was definitely offended, but her brother's antics generated some mirth.

"*What?* I've always been curious, and now I know someone in the business."

"Ugh. Fine. I haven't been with a true professional porn star, so I can't speak to how the pros are equipped. These guys are...on the high side of average. One guy might have been seven inches. Maybe. I've only been with nine guys so far."

Pat huffed. "I'm so disappointed. Also, nine? In five weeks? Don't you have a busy little beaver?"

"*Pat.*"

"What? I'm impressed. I mean, rookie numbers compared to my college days, but still."

"I don't need to hear how slutty my brother was in college."

His voice lost its flirty touch. "Seriously, Livvy. If you need something, just ask. People in L.A. pay stupid amounts of money for my art. *Stupid.* It's kind of embarrassing, actually."

"I'm fine for now, Pat. But, thank you. I will keep your offer in mind."

"You do that. I love you, Livvy."

"I love you, too, Pat. I need to go. Give my love to Bruce."

Pat chuckled, his tone playfully horny. "All night long."

"Oh, my God. I'm hanging up now." Talking with Pat was a welcome breath of fresh air. Olivia needed to tell someone about her secret double life, and he was probably the only person on the planet who she trusted not to judge her. *Plus, now I won't feel so compelled to spill my guts to Cathy.*

It was a week and a half until the Valentine's Day doubleheader in New York. She'd see Maxim then, get this mess sorted out, and get the wedding back on track.

Those intervening days came and went with wins against Pittsburgh, Montréal, and Detroit, and an overtime loss to Chicago. The Blossoms arrived in New York the day before Valentine's Day. Olivia informed the team travel coordinator that she didn't need a hotel room since she would stay with her fiancé. Maxim seemed off when she arrived at his condo, avoiding eye contact, and not initiating sex. The latter was both concerning and a relief. Olivia knew that Maxim always wanted sex before games. It was part of his ritual, and hockey players are notoriously superstitious.

The women's game was the first part of the doubleheader, so Olivia left early for the arena. She turned off her phone because she didn't want to engage with the torrent of texts from her mother, all about Maxim. The first period was rocky as Olivia struggled to get her head in the game.

Keisha sidled up beside her as they walked back from the locker room. "What is wrong with you, bitch? This fucking team traded you. Get your shit together, and show them why they made a mistake."

Olivia shook her head in silence. As the seconds ticked down toward the second period, the announcer loudly directed the entire arena's eyes to the jumbotron for the Kiss Cam. Without thinking, Olivia looked up, and there in a skybox, on camera for the world to see, was her fiancé with his tongue down another woman's throat and his hand up her shirt.

"Well, that's not very family-friendly. Sorry, folks." The announcer's voice boomed. "But it sure looks like Maxim Kovalev is about to score off the ice while his fiancée is still scoreless on the ice."

There was no way to know for certain if twenty thousand pairs of eyes were staring at you at once, but it certainly felt like they were to Olivia. More than anything in the world, she wanted to find a hole, crawl into it, and never come out again. She felt a firm touch on her right arm, then another hand on her chin, raising her head so she looked directly at Cathy.

Her normally ebullient friend's face was blotchy with incandescent rage. Blazing eyes shone under neon pink hair. Cathy growled, "Fuck New York." From behind her, Hicks echoed the sentiment, loud enough for the entire bench to hear, "Fuck New York." The rest of her teammates—even Keisha—chorused, "Fuck New York."

Olivia felt her spirits tremble in the cold darkness of her shame. The entire team banged their sticks on the boards as Olivia's line took the ice, their fury lifting her from the abyss. Still unfocused, Olivia lost the opening face-off of the second half, but it didn't matter. Cathy obliterated the defender as she tried to corral the puck. Taking possession, the pink-haired demon raced toward the net, feinting a shot and sliding the rubber across the crease, where Olivia buried it in the back of the net.

She felt her blood racing as the team roared their affirmation when her line returned to the bench. Misty's line surged onto the ice with wicked gleams in their eyes. Over the next forty minutes, the enraged Blossoms made New York atone in blood and tears for humiliating Olivia on the Kiss Cam.

After the game, the team took Olivia out for a drink, with Hicks announcing the first round was on the Blossoms. Svetlana called out, "At New York prices? Caine's gonna flip."

Hicks grinned. "Trust me, I know."

Olivia saw Cathy talking to Keisha before they entered the bar. Cathy squeezed Keisha's hand before Keisha walked off into the night. "What were you two talking about?"

Cathy shrugged. "Keisha didn't feel like celebrating with you. Plus she has a Valentine's night hookup."

"I'm not sure I'm really celebrating. My engagement is probably over."

Her pink-haired friend grinned with a sparkle in her eyes. "Liv, you don't need him. He's a cheating asshole. You should *definitely* celebrate the end of your engagement."

"It's complicated, Cat. Very complicated."

"Come on inside, have a drink, and bask in the team's support. Maybe things will be less complicated."

As much as Olivia appreciated the camaraderie, she felt emotionally drained. She truly appreciated their support, especially Cathy's. As players broke off to chat with each other or address overtures from strangers, Olivia considered leaving. She put her hand on Cathy's shoulder to get her attention. "Hey, Cat. I'm heading out."

Concern filled Cathy's expression. "Where are you going to stay?"

"I don't know. I'll figure something out."

"No, I have a great idea. Why don't you sleep in Keisha's bed? Trust me, she won't need it tonight."

"How can you be sure?"

Olivia watched Cathy's eyebrows shoot up. "Oh yeah, I'm positive. That woman is a pussy-seeking missile. When she goes out to get laid, she doesn't come back until breakfast."

"Okay, thanks, and wow..." She couldn't restrain the laugh bubbling up from her gut. "I don't think I'll ever be able to look at Keisha taking a slap shot the same way."

"Here." Cathy reached into the pocket of her jeans. "Take my spare keycard. I'm going out dancing, so I'll see you much later. You're the bed on the right."

Olivia hugged her friend. "Be safe. Have a great time. Watch your drink. And thank you again, Cat. You're a good friend."

"Of course. Have a good night, Liv."

Inside the hotel room, Olivia scampered into the bathroom. After tonight—knowing everything she'd done to maintain this sham of an engagement was for naught—she felt unclean on a level far deeper than her skin. Olivia stripped off her clothes and stepped into the shower, wishing the running water would slough off her shame and guilt.

Chapter 14

Girls Girls Girls

Fletcher

Keisha stormed across the hotel lobby, fingering her keycard as she approached the elevators. Slashing her card across the reader, she waited impatiently for the doors to open. Keisha pounded the button for her floor, buried a scream, then stabbed her keycard against the interior reader until an indicator light turned green. Exasperated, she punched the button for her floor again, hissing as the elevator doors closed.

"I love your hair, is it natural?" Bitch, is yours, cuz it looks like it came out of a discount bottle. "Wow, a Black hockey player. How come you didn't play basketball?" "You people have such nice skin." "Are you sure your hair's not a weave?" "I wish I had your skin. Then I'd be tan all the time."

The last remark from the ignorant woman put Keisha over the top. She wanted to get laid, but not enough to endure an entire evening of listening to an idiot.

It's Valentine's Day in New York City. There must be at least a thousand other lesbians looking for a one night stand tonight. Why did I have to pick the damn blonde? I've been picking way too many blondes recently, and I don't know why. Whatever. I'm gonna change into something sexier, swipe on literally anyone who isn't a fucking blonde, and get some horizontal action tonight.

Keisha stomped out of the elevator, turning toward her room. She swiped the keycard and entered, surprised to hear the shower running. "Hey, Cat. I didn't expect you back so soon."

Maybe she pulled someone. Nice, Cat. Get some dick tonight.

She didn't see anyone else and shrugged her shoulders. *Whatever. I'll change real fast.* The water shut off, but the fan was running. Deciding against further attempts at conversation, Keisha pulled on a dress and heels, idly swiping through potential hookups. *No more blondes.*

Keisha looked up as the bathroom door opened, and a blonde woman wrapped in a towel stepped out. *Olivia.* "What the fuck are you doing here, bitch?"

Olivia screamed and scrabbled at her towel before it fell to the floor. "Me? Cathy said you'd be out all night."

"Doesn't answer the question of why you're here," Keisha snapped.

"Because I can't go back to Maxim's," Olivia shouted.

Keisha stood up, fists balled at her sides. "Oh yeah, your boyfriend was sucking face with some other whore," she sneered. "Looks like he's trading up, tramp."

"I'm—" Olivia froze.

"What? Not a whore? Can princesses even be whores? Probably. It seems like they're bred to spread their legs for rich bastards. Is that how Mommy and Daddy raised you, Puck Princess? To open your thighs for some Russian prick? I mean prince?" Keisha's laugh brimmed with condescension.

"Please. Stop," her rival wailed.

"Aw, bitch can't take it? Maybe you should have stopped before you tried to put me in the ground." Keisha's fist came up. "Why don't you go get yourself the Princess suite over at the Four Seasons?" Her arm cocked back as she readied to swing.

"Please. Stop." The fog of rage parted just enough for Keisha to notice Olivia crying. Not just crying. Bawling. "Please," the blonde whimpered. "I'm sorry. Sorry for everything. I'm begging you to stop."

Keisha's fist lowered. Punching Olivia right now would be like kicking a puppy. Keisha might hate Olivia, but the kinder side of her couldn't bear to see someone weeping. "Why are you crying?" Her voice was softer, although still ragged.

"Besides my now ex-fiancé getting it on in a skybox with someone else?"

"Is there more?"

"Yeah, there's a lot fucking more," Olivia briefly raged before breaking once again into snotty whimpers. "I'm up to my ears in debt. My family is broke. Maxim's dad is loaded with Russian mob money, and the only reason I even agreed to marry him was to help my family out. So congratu-fucking-lations, Keisha. You're absolutely right that I'm a princess and a whore."

Keisha felt like she'd been kicked. She'd meant those words to cause pain, not realizing they might be true.

"I spread my legs for a worthless cheating prick so his daddy's mob money could save my parents the embarrassment of going bankrupt. But the shame doesn't stop there. Oh no, not for the Puck Princess. I live in a shitty studio apartment, because I'm broke."

"But your clothes…"

"Yes, I maxed out credit cards to buy expensive clothes to create this image of success so I could land the Russian mob prince. Shopping also makes me feel good, which I realize is an addictive problem, which I'm working on."

The blonde woman threw her hands in the air, her face a mask of defeat and utter humiliation. "Do you know how I've been paying rent, buying food, and finally starting to pay down my credit card bills? Porn. I've been fucking guys on camera to pay for my fucking clothes for something that—" Olivia fell silent, beating her head with her fists. "*AAAAHHHH!*" The scream ripped from her throat.

Keisha stood in shocked silence as Olivia blubbered in front of her.

"I'm a whore twice over and for nothing. *Nothing.* I hate my life. I hate myself for what I did to you. I'm sorry, Keisha. I'm so fucking sorry. You were incredible. Beautiful. I took everything away from you because I'm a worthless, jealous bitch. You are still fantastic.

Every time I step onto the ice with you, it's fucking magic. Please, just punch me. Kick me. Beat the living shit out of me, I don't care. I deserve it. I deserve everything you do to me and so much more." Olivia's body was wracked with more sobs as she buried her face in her hands.

Reflexively, Keisha's hands reached out, pulling Olivia close. Somewhere inside her head, a tiny voice was screaming, *What the hell?* Keisha stuffed the annoying little voice back a bit deeper. She'd worry about her hate later. Right now she felt pity.

She also felt wet. The front of her dress was soaking wet. Keisha gingerly slid a hand down past Olivia's shoulders to discover the other woman's towel was gone.

Olivia nudged Keisha back. Her eyes were red and puffy. "Why aren't you hitting me?"

Keisha's eyes flicked down to take in Olivia's small, perfect breasts. Bringing her eyes back up, she said, "I'm still considering it." Keisha's eyes widened in surprise as Olivia leaned forward, planting a light kiss on her lips.

"What the fuck?"

Olivia reeled back. "I'm sorry. I'm so sorry. I've been thinking about it since the night at the strip club."

Keisha's mind struggled to adjust to yet another new piece of information. "Wait. *What?*"

"I tried stripping for a few weeks to make some quick cash. You came in with your blue-haired girlfriend. Oh no, I don't want to mess that up."

"Holy shit. *You* were the stripper?"

"Yes." The blonde nodded, her cheeks blazing pink.

"Wow." Suddenly, it wasn't just Keisha's outer clothes that were wet. "What were you thinking?"

"Mostly, I was terrified you would recognize me. But your lips felt good. Wonderful, actually. I didn't let myself think of your lips before, but yeah. Wonderful is a good description."

"I'm not sure what to say."

Olivia must have realized she was naked, because she covered up those tantalizing tits, turning away. "I should go."

Keisha reached out to grasp Olivia's arm and pulled, whipping her around. Face to face, Keisha jammed her other hand into the blonde hair at the nape of Olivia's neck and grabbed a fistful. She pressed her lips against Olivia's, sensing her initial shock, then acceptance, and finally, fervent reciprocation. Their hands roamed freely, Keisha thoroughly enjoying Olivia's damp and naked skin. The other woman tugged at Keisha's dress, whimpering into her mouth.

She stepped back, panting. Olivia pulled at Keisha's dress again. "Please?" She mewled. Keisha helped Olivia shimmy the dress off her body. Olivia breathed, "You're beautiful."

"Thank you."

Keisha watched Olivia's eyes travel downward until they reached her leg. Those eyes widened as she took in the scar tissue there.

"Oh, fuck," she said, her voice cracking. "Keisha, I'm so sorry."

She pulled Olivia's chin up. "Hey. Let's not talk about the past right now."

Olivia bobbed her head. "I've never...been with a woman before."

Keisha purred, "It's just like with a man, but better, because I know what the hell I'm doing." The blonde groaned, burying her face into Keisha's chest. "Since you're down there..." She felt Oivia's tongue tentatively brush a nipple, which immediately pebbled in response. Keisha moaned as Olivia licked her nipple again with more confidence. Soon, the other woman was licking and nibbling delightfully. "I've got another one..." Keisha reminded her. Olivia took the hint.

Keisha kicked off her heels and used a free hand to yank her panties down. Gravity took care of the rest. Fully unencumbered, Keisha edged them both toward the bed before falling backward. Olivia squeaked as Keisha pulled her onto the mattress. Their mouths met again. Keisha was taken aback by the suddenly ferocious hunger consuming Olivia as their mouths merged and tongues melded. Olivia climbed on top of Keisha, grinding her pelvis down desperately.

She felt Olivia's wetness as she humped Keisha's muscular thigh. Olivia's left hand slid under Keisha's neck while her right hand snaked urgently down to Keisha's hungry pussy. Her fingers danced across the opening, gathering lubrication. Keisha groaned into Olivia's mouth as she fed a finger inside. Then a second finger. Then she curled her fingers upward. Olivia pumped her hand like a dying woman at a well.

"Shhh, slow it down. It's not a race."

Adjusting her pace, Olivia continued thrusting, palm pressed hard against Keisha's clit. She reveled in the obscene and glorious squelching coming from her saturated pussy. Keisha reached a hand over to cup one of Olivia's boobs, tweaking a pink nipple.

Keisha craned up to kiss Olivia, indulging in her cute cries of pleasure. She felt her own rapture rising as Olivia's continued caresses did their job. Keisha whimpered into Olivia's mouth as she sawed and scissored Keisha's wet walls. Olivia's fingertips stroked Keisha's g-spot, sending hedonistic tremors up her spine and straight into her brain.

She felt her breath getting shorter, more ragged. Keisha couldn't focus enough to kiss Olivia anymore, and her hands fell to her sides as she gripped the sheets, holding on like they were the last thing connecting her to Earth.

"Oh. Olivia, yes, Oh. Oh—" Keisha came undone, back arching as she screamed wordless syllables into the night. She lay on her back, panting and staring at the ceiling. Olivia leaned over to kiss her tenderly, slowly withdrawing her right hand. Keisha whipped her left hand up with the speed of a striking mongoose to grip Olivia's hand. She brought that hand up to Olivia's mouth and fed those sopping fingers in. Olivia moaned around her hand, tongue licking each digit clean.

"Do you want to learn how to eat pussy?"

Olivia keened softly as her head bobbed in impassioned affirmation.

Keisha scooted up the bed, adjusting the pillows to comfortably elevate her head and pelvis. She placed a hand between her thighs and beckoned Olivia. "I want you to explore me with your tongue. How I feel, how I taste. Ohh." Olivia's tongue teased her labia, gently parting her lower lips. She traced tentatively up, tickling and teasing Keisha's clit.

Olivia planted her lips firmly around Keisha's pearl and sucked while still circling with her tongue. Keisha hissed as teeth nibbled gently. She sank her fingers deep into the mop of blonde hair bobbing between her thighs, tilting Olivia's head and almost losing herself in the cerulean ocean of her eyes. She felt a rush at the adoration reflected in her rival's gaze. "You're doing so good," Keisha affirmed, reveling in the physical sensations and the power.

The licks and flicks slowed down, haphazard in their aim and effect. "When your tongue gets tired, switch to kisses. Also, use your head, neck, and back to reduce fatigue," Keisha instructed. The blonde head bobbed and tilted, sweat sticking her hair to her forehead. A flat tongue traversed Keisha's cleft from bottom to top as Olivia absorbed her lessons.

Supple fingers delved into the steamy recesses of her core as Olivia's tongue lashed her clitoris. Her thighs quivered as she built toward her crescendo. Keisha's tongue flicked across her lips while she drew in a ragged breath. Her hands clenched into fists, spurring renewed efforts at the apex of her thighs.

Keisha howled into oblivion, her body shuddering as the waves of pleasure threatened to drown her. She curled upward, breath caught in her throat. Explosions of ecstasy were all she knew.

Tender, tangy kisses woke Keisha. Her eyelids fluttered open to perceive Olivia's sodden face before her. *I think I blacked out.* She traced her fingertips up Olivia's arms, relishing the goosebumps she elicited. Olivia mewled when the fingertips reached her neck, shivering with a smile. She cupped the other woman's face, drawing her downward for a deep, sensual kiss.

Olivia eventually settled herself in the crook of Keisha's arm, one pale hand idly toying with a dark nipple. "Did I do well?"

"You were very good. Especially for a rookie."

She giggled and cuddled tighter.

Keisha lay on her back, staring at the ceiling as the orgasmic afterglow faded. A memory surfaced of lying on her back on another bed long ago, courtesy of a blindside hit. *What the hell am I doing? I just had sex with Olivia Fucking Kennedy. Technically, she had sex with me since I'm the only one who got off.* Her hand meandered down Olivia's back to the curve of her pert ass. *There's a certain justice to having her fuck me to multiple orgasms while I give her nothing. Then again, I have a once in a lifetime opportunity to* ruin *her. I'll give her a high that she'll spend the rest of her life chasing.* She felt a wicked grin spread across her face as she rolled Olivia on her back, fingers seeking her blonde bush. *Oh yeah. I'm going to make the Puck Princess* beg.

Chapter 15

Living The Lie

Dio

The sound of running water woke Olivia. She was in an unfamiliar bed, and her back felt hot and sweaty. The sound of running water shut off, replaced by soft footfalls on carpet. Olivia cracked an eyelid to illuminate Cathy standing next to the bed in boy shorts and a Blossoms t-shirt, staring at her in stark disbelief. *If Cathy is standing there, then... Oh, fuck. Last night wasn't a dream. Or rather, an intensely sexual and pleasurable nightmare.*

Hearing a soft snore behind her, Olivia stealthily slipped out of bed. Cathy's eyes widened, and she realized she was buck naked in front of her only friend. Covering herself as best she could, Olivia scuttled to retrieve her clothes. Once dressed, she tipped her head toward the door. Cathy followed her into the hallway.

"What the hell, Liv?" Cathy palmed her forehead, eyes wide. "I mean seriously. *What. The. Hell?* You're *sleeping* with Keisha? Last time I checked, the two of you couldn't be in the same room together, much less *naked* in a bed."

"Any chance you wanna get breakfast? And coffee? This might take a while, and I would very much prefer not to have this conversation standing in this hallway."

"Fine. There's a deli a couple blocks away."

"What about the hotel?"

"Breakfast here costs as much as my rent. Trust me, the deli is better."

Olivia didn't need to consider the miserable state of her bank account before agreeing. They hurried through the frigid February air, reaching the deli before their toes froze. She considered what a strange pair they made—Cathy in Blossoms sweats and her in last night's rumpled clothing.

Cathy moaned on the stool next to her. "This bagel smells amazing. You, on the other hand, smell like sweat and sex. Let me have a few bites to enjoy this delicacy before you tell me whatever sordid tale you've got."

She took this opportunity to delight in her own bagel and coffee, heartbeat accelerating as the first molecules of caffeine entered her system. Olivia licked the last dab of cream cheese off her finger, remembering the previous night's activities. She stared morosely at her empty bagel wrapper, as she contemplated getting another when Cathy interrupted her thoughts.

"Ahem. Time to spill."

"First, let me say I'm sorry for not telling you a lot of this before. You've been a good friend, and I've never been fully honest with you before."

"It's okay, Liv. You can tell me anything."

"I hope you don't hate me after this." Olivia told Cathy everything. Her family's financial troubles, her parents kicking Patrick out for being gay, the arrangement to marry Maxim for his family's money, the humiliation of Maxim's incessant cheating, his pathetic bedroom skills, and then finally her own recent struggles with money and foray into porn.

"Wow, Liv. That's a *lot*."

"No shit," said a voice behind them.

Olivia whipped around to discover Daniella, Heike, and Svetlana sitting at a small table directly behind her. The trio stared at her, their breakfasts cooling on the table. "Oh, fuck. How long have you been there?"

Svetlana hitched her shoulders. "From when you said your parents were broke. By the way, the Kovalevs are dangerous. Maxim might be an idiot, but his father is not."

"So you heard about..."

All three nodded.

"I'm going to be sick." Olivia's legs felt like sticks of warm butter. Being unsure of whether she could actually stand was the only thing preventing her from running screaming down the street.

Daniella stood up to embrace Olivia. "It's okay. We're not going to tell anyone. *Comprende.*"

Heike shrugged. "I'm German. Posting homemade sex videos is a national pastime."

Svetlana giggled. "I was born in Russia, even if I grew up in Brooklyn. Charging people for homemade sex videos is half of my erstwhile homeland's economy."

Cathy placed a comforting hand on Olivia's arm. "I'm your friend, so your secret is safe with me. You still haven't told me how you ended up sleeping with Keisha."

Olivia almost giggled when three jaws dropped in unison. "I was getting to it."

"More like getting some," Cathy snickered.

"Hush, or I won't tell you what happened."

Daniella poked her in the chest with a finger. "Oh no. We've gotta hear this."

Olivia leaned against the counter. "I wasn't in a good place last night. You know, with the whole Maxim debacle. Cathy offered me a bed to sleep in because Keisha had a date and wouldn't need the bed. A 'pussy-seeking missile' was the term she used to describe Keisha. I went to the room and took a shower. I just felt so dirty and guilty after finding out my engagement was over. Anyway, I walked out of the bathroom in a towel and Keisha was there. I guess her date bombed. She started yelling at me and I yelled back, but then I started crying. I'm bawling my eyes out, she's about to punch me, and then...she doesn't. Instead she asked why I'm crying."

She spun around to grip her cup of coffee. Taking a sip did nothing to moisten her suddenly dry mouth, but it gave her space to compose herself. Twisting back to her audience, Olivia rasped. "I…" She swallowed before trying again. "I…"

Svetlana told her to wait and strode off to get water. The towering Russian returned with a bottle, passing it to Olivia. She took a deep swig, swishing the parched feeling away.

"Thank you. As I was saying, I broke down and told Keisha everything you all eavesdropped on. Then I told her I'm sorry for what I've done to her." Olivia gulped more water.

"The wait is killing me," Daniella snapped.

"Sorry, Daniella."

The raven-haired Latina snickered. "We're at the point in our relationship where we're talking about your sex life. You can call me Dani."

"Thanks." Olivia took another swig. "I told Keisha what a whore I am, and how I'm sorry for hurting her, then she hugged me."

"She voluntarily hugged you?" Heike sounded unconvinced.

"I don't think she believed it, either. So yeah, she hugged me, and then I kissed her. Like, just a little kiss. I panicked, and then suddenly we were making out. Somewhere along the way we ended up naked. Actually, I think my towel fell when Keisha hugged me, so I was already naked."

"Aren't you straight?" Cathy pointed out.

"Yes. Maybe? I'm not thinking straight right now."

Svetlana snorted. "Thinking gay, maybe." Olivia's teammates all chuckled.

"I haven't processed last night at all."

Dani leaned in, but her whisper was more than loud enough. "Was it good?"

Olivia shuddered. "Holy shit. It was *amazing.* I've never cum so hard in my entire life. Keisha seemed to enjoy it as well. I think I might have blacked out. Her fingers and tongue did things to me I never knew were possible."

Her face was suddenly suffused with rose hair and Cathy's voice in her ear. "I'm so happy for you, Liv." Through the fringes of pink, she could see her teammates' shocked faces morph into grins, then everyone joined in for a group hug with a chorus of "Wows" and other affirmations. The unconditional support of her teammates lifted Olivia's spirits. Combined with a night of incredible sex, she was feeling better than she had in a while.

Cathy and Olivia waited for the other three to finish their breakfasts before the whole group trudged back to the hotel. "Where's your stuff?" Svetlana asked along the way.

"Still at Maxim's," she groaned. "Ugh. I should just leave it."

"Nope," Dani intoned. "Let us get changed, and we'll come with you."

"You all don't have to get involved with my problems."

Heike's grin was lopsided, toothy, and more than a bit feral. "It will be fun." She high-fived her defensive partner.

"Thank you. I'll just wait here in the lobby," Olivia said before she watched her teammates amble over to the elevator. She pulled out her phone once she was alone.

Her brother whined, "Livvy, do you know what time it is?"

"Sorry, I'm in New York. I forgot."

"It's fine. You obviously have something urgent to tell me."

"I slept with someone last night, Pat." She didn't bother to contain the glee in her voice.

"You sound happy about sex, so I assume it wasn't Moron."

"Maxim."

"Whatever. Was it one of your porn studs? He must have been amazing."

"*No.* It wasn't a guy from"—Olivia lowered her voice—my side hustle."

"Oh, hooking up with strange men in New York. Livvy, I'm impressed."

"Pat, shush. I didn't hook up with a *man*." She waited, giggling at the gasp on the other end of the line.

"*No... Yes.* Livvy...did you dine at the Y?"

"What does dining at the Y even mean? Oh, wait. I get it now."

"You had sex with a woman? How was it? I have so many questions. Sweetie, my sister is a muff diver. Bruce is awake now, too, and he has questions."

"Oh my God. Pat, you have to stop. Yes, I had sex with a woman, and it was the absolute best sex I've ever had. But, it wasn't just *any* woman."

"Livvy, who was it?"

"Keisha Owens," she crowed, then looked guiltily around the lobby.

Patrick gasped. "What the fuck. She hates you."

"After last night—"

"Have you talked to her?"

"No, but I'm sure it's fine. I apologized."

Pat sounded unconvinced. "Oh. Okay. You said I'm sorry, then fucked, and everything is fine now. Two decades worth of bad blood is simply gone because of pussy magic."

"You're being unfair."

"Livvy. I love you to pieces, and I desperately want you to be right about Keisha."

"But you don't think so," Olivia responded flatly.

"I'm sorry, Livvy. I don't."

Tears welled in her eyes. "I thought you'd be happy for me."

"Sweetheart. I'm overjoyed to hear about your forays into exploring your sexuality. I'll be ecstatic if you dump your useless prick of a fiancé. But this…I worry about you." Olivia heard the genuine concern in her brother's voice.

"Thank you."

"Now, onto the important things. Are you done with men? Going to swing both ways? Or, was this a one-time thing?"

"Slow down. I honestly don't know. Last night was incredible. She did things—"

"Livvy, do I tell you details of my bedroom adventures?"

"No."

"Then please, skip the play-by-play."

"Sorry. I am still processing this, but I will try to keep any details from my poor brother's sensitive ears. Anyway. No man has ever made me feel like she did. You know. Down there. But, I didn't feel any emotional connection." She stopped to reconsider. "That's not true. I did for a second, right at the beginning." Olivia recalled those first couple of kisses, then what followed. "Oh shit, Pat. Now, I'm worried you're right. How do I manage to screw everything up in my life?"

"Maybe I'm wrong. Talk to me. Tell me about the connection."

"I was so messed up. She looked at me differently. Not as her enemy or the person who fucked up her entire life, but as a person. The walls came down, and I kissed her. She was startled, I think. We kissed again. It felt like we were just one being. Then we fell on the bed and somewhere around then, it wasn't the same."

"All right, you had a moment. Connection is important. Talk to her."

"I will." The elevator doors opened, disgorging her teammates. "Pat, I gotta go. Some of the Blossoms are helping me get my stuff from Maxim's."

"Good luck. Have you told Mom and Dad?"

"*Oh fuck.*"

"You've got this, Livvy. No matter what, I love you."

"Thanks, Pat. Your love and support helps more than I can express. Bye for now."

Her friends swarmed around her, cheerfully encouraging her as the group made their way to the street. They piled into a nearby subway station for the short ride to Maxim's. Olivia waved to the doorman. "Hey, Claude."

"Miss Olivia, you shouldn't—"

"It's fine, Claude. I know he's got another woman up there. I'm just getting my stuff and leaving."

"I should call up."

"Of course. I would expect nothing less."

The doorman reached for the phone as Olivia led her posse to the elevator. "We'll give him a second." She waited until Claude was speaking before opening the elevator. It was crowded with five hockey players inside. "Claude's a good guy. I don't want him to get in trouble," Olivia explained. She led them to Maxim's door. He threw it open before she touched the door knob.

"Why are you here?"

"I'm getting my shit. We're done." She could see the bimbo from last night in the background wearing nothing but a pink babydoll. "Don't be an idiot and let me in."

True to form, Maxim was an idiot. "Nyet."

Olivia felt her friends behind her. Svetlana was slightly taller than Maxim, and Heike was the same height. Glancing to each side, she read the determined expressions on their faces. While Maxim wildly shifted his eyes from face to face, Olivia punched him in the nuts. "You could have just said, 'Da,' you fucking moron," she growled as she stormed past.

Dani and Cat kept Maxim's new girlfriend from interfering while Heike and Svetlana babysat her ex. She grabbed her bag, stuffing her clothes inside. Walking to the bookcase, she pulled select books off the shelf and retrieved the dildos and vibrators secreted behind. Those went in her bag as well. Zipping it up, she stalked out the door, her friends in tow. She didn't bother to bid her ex farewell.

In the lobby, she called out, "Goodbye, Claude. I'll miss you."

"I will miss you, too, Miss Olivia. I don't like the new girlfriend at all."

"She'll warm up to you, I'm sure. Thank you."

"Goodbye, Miss Olivia."

In the subway, Dani asked, "You kept your toys stashed on the bookshelf?"

Olivia snorted. "It's the one place Maxim was guaranteed to never look." They all chuckled.

They returned in time for everyone to be packed and ready for the bus ride to the airport. Olivia found Keisha off to the side of the hotel lobby. "Hi."

The other woman whipped around. "What is it?" Keisha snarled.

Her hands came up defensively. "Oh, I—"

"What? You thought one night of below average sex would make up for everything? Maybe you forgot you're straight. Or did you think last night turned you into a lesbian?"

The ferocity in Keisha's voice shocked Olivia. She mustered a stumbling response. "We had a moment."

"A moment?" Keisha's sneer was matched by the derision dripping in her tone. "I didn't feel any moment. All I know is I took pity on a blubbering bitch. That's all last night was. Pity sex. You're welcome."

The earth fell away, and Olivia plummeted into the abyss, fighting the tears welling in her eyes. She held her head up and gathered what little of her shredded dignity was left. "I guess I owe you a thank you, then. And fuck you for being such a horrible bitch." She planted her heel and wheeled away to stalk across the lobby. Seeing the restrooms, she fled inside where she collapsed on a toilet. Alone, her will crumbled and tears flowed undammed down her cheeks.

Olivia wallowed in misery and humiliation, her darkness exacerbated by lingering memories of Keisha's lips and fingertips.

Chapter 16

Wicked Game

Chris Isaak

Her ass is perfect. Keisha thought as her gaze followed Olivia across the hotel lobby. *Taut, muscular, with a curvature that fills those leggings like they were painted on. It felt so good in my hands. Which is why she's walking away. The sex was incredible, but I was hate-fucking her. It didn't mean anything—doesn't change anything. She's still the bitch who almost disabled me. Damn me if her lips didn't feel like they were made for me, though. Nope. I can't think about her lips. Last night was a one-time thing. A mistake. A glorious, magical mistake. It won't happen again. "I'm sorry" doesn't fix relearning to walk and skate. It sure as hell doesn't fix missing the Olympics or a decade of professional hockey. Her apologies and train wreck of a life mean nothing to me. Even if her kisses were immacu-*

late. Fuck. I have to stop thinking about Olivia fucking Kennedy. Or fucking Olivia Kennedy. All of the above.

Keisha cringed when she observed Cathy walking toward her.

She was her typical effervescent self. "Good morning. How are you?"

"I'm fine," Keisha grunted.

"Just *fine?*" Her tone teased at the truth. "Because you looked so cozy in your bed this morning...with Olivia."

"I don't want to talk about it."

She watched the light dim in her friend's eyes.

Fuck. I'm such an asshole.

"Oh."

"Look, Cat. It's not what you think. Well, it sort of is. Anyway, I made a huge mistake last night, but it's no big deal."

"Which is it? A huge mistake or no big deal?" Her friend's voice had a hard steel edge now.

"Why do you care?" Keisha didn't mean to sound harsh, but she winced when she saw Cathy flinch.

"I care because you're my friend, Keisha. Liv is my friend, too." Her voice rose. "And you were in bed together, which kinda seems like a big...fucking...deal."

"It's not. I don't even see how you can be friends with both of us."

"Because—" Cathy grunted, balling her fists. "Actually, never mind. I'm not playing whatever game this is." Her hands unclenched and her voice softened. "Whenever you are ready to talk, I'm here for you. Because I *am* your friend. And if you don't want to talk with me, then talk with someone else."

"I don't need to talk about anything."

"Okay. Sure. Whatever." The disappointment in Cathy's voice was deep. "I'm here when you change your mind." Cathy shook her head and meandered back to the rest of the team.

Keisha regarded her retreating form. *I'm being a bitch, but she had no right to go poking into things. She's acting like Olivia and I have feelings for each other. I'm pretty sure that bitch only cares about herself. As for me...nah. I've got nothing but hate for that cheapshotting whore. I need to stop thinking of her.*

She hurried over to Hicks. "Hey. Coach. You want to go over some film together?"

Chapter 17

True Colors

Cyndi Lauper

Olivia texted Pat to tell him he was right, then resumed weeping in the restroom stall. Her phone rang and she picked up without looking.

"Pat?"

Her mother's angry voice blared out of the receiver instead. "No, it's your parents. What the fuck is going on, Olivia? We heard you broke your engagement to Maxim."

"He has a girlfriend, Mom, so he kind of already broke it. Also, I'm done with being humiliated by him."

"This is much bigger than you, pumpkin," her father chimed in. "Now is not the time to be selfish. This marriage is important to our family."

Isn't this just fucking wonderful. They're on speaker so they can both badger me at once.

"*No.* It's important to you two, not the family."

"You're part of this family," her mother harrumphed. "And your family needs you."

"Your mother is right."

"Oh, and what about when I need you? Do you call and tell me what a good job I did when I had a good game, or to support me if I don't? No. All I ever get from you is Maxim, Maxim, Maxim."

"Honey—"

"I'm done prostituting myself to some ignorant sack of shit because of your bad decisions. I've let him abuse and humiliate me for two years now, for your fucking benefit, and I'm not doing it anymore. I'm done. I'm out. If you want Maxim's money so bad, then why don't you have Mom fuck him?"

"*Olivia Isabella Kennedy.*" Her father's voice cracked like a whip. "Watch your tone when speaking to your parents, you ungrateful whelp."

"Why? What are you going to do? Cut me off? Disinherit me? From what love or money? Are you going to ignore me and treat me like shit? Oh wait, you already do." She couldn't keep the sneer out of her voice, and she didn't care.

"That's not true," her mother pleaded.

"Like hell. When was the last time you talked to me without mentioning Maxim? When I played in Minneapolis, did you come meet me at the airport?" The memory of seeing Keisha with her mother still grated. She wanted the same kind of parental love, but knew her parents were incapable of it. "Or watch my game? No. You didn't."

"We were busy."

"Busy with what? What was so important for you to ignore your own daughter? You know who supports me? Pat. Pat calls me—"

Her father growled, "We don't say his name."

"*I do.* Pat loves me. He actually listens to me."

"Oh, now I see how it is. The little faggot is finally getting his revenge."

"Fuck you, Dad. So what if he's gay? At least he's happy."

"Until he burns in Hell."

"Then I'll gladly keep him company."

Silence. Ponderous, palpable silence, broken only by her father's strenuous breathing.

Her mother finally whispered, "What do you mean?"

Olivia wiped the tears from her eyes, sitting up straight on the toilet. Finding her dignity in a public restroom with smudged cheeks and clothes stained from her earlier tears was no easy task, but she gathered what she could. Her voice was haggard as she announced, "I slept with a woman last night."

They don't need to know how Keisha rejected me. I can keep one piece of my shame to myself.

Rage permeated her father's inflection. "You're a dyke now? A carpet munching lesbo. After all we've done for you. Raised you. Trained you. Protected you from your own fuck ups. *And this is how you repay us.*" Olivia heard her mother feebly attempting to calm him down. "If you love your faggot brother so much, then go be with him. I won't tolerate your deviance and sin, you ungrateful slut."

Unwilling to listen to her father's tirade, she hung up. When they called back, she blocked their number. She was puzzled by her lack of tears. Somehow, potentially ending her relationship with her parents was less heart-wrenching than Keisha's rejection. Olivia contemplated her conundrum all the way to the airport.

Embarking on the plane, Olivia studiously avoided looking at Keisha. She stumbled her way to the back of the plane, stowing her bag and taking the aisle seat. Cathy arrived immediately behind her, clambering over Olivia's legs to take the window seat. Svetlana was right behind Cathy. "Scoot over, please," the giant Russian rumbled. Olivia grumbled and unhooked her seat belt before hopping into the middle. Dani, Heike, and Sophie claimed the three seats in front of them while Svetlana was settling her big frame into the aisle seat.

Cathy leaned over, asking, "Lana, are you excited to see Sebastian when we get back?"

Three heads in front inclined simultaneously to hear the answer. Svetlana's face and neck blossomed a rosy pink. "Yes. He's planning a special surprise for me."

The pink-haired woman squeed in delight. "What is it?"

"A surprise. Ask Dani, she's his sister."

Dani grunted from the next row up, "Don't look at me. Sebastian hasn't told me anything. It's weird enough knowing he's banging my goalie."

Svetlana's face darkened from pink to scarlet.

Heike snickered, "I hope he doesn't put a biscuit in her basket."

Olivia hadn't thought Svetlana could get any redder, but she did.

Dani threw her hands in the air. "Please don't make me think about my brother knocking my friend up."

A slight squeak from Svetlana drew Olivia's attention. She kept her mouth shut, unsure what to make of the noise.

Sophie popped her head up. "Kennedy, what's going on with you and Owens?"

Olivia glared at her friends. "Nothing, why?" She answered cautiously.

The captain chortled. "I was in the next room. I'm *very* well aware that *something* happened between the two of you. Based on the amount of noise, there was either a brawl or the two-backed-beast, and I'm fairly certain you wouldn't have screamed 'Oh. Yes. Keisha. Don't stop' if she were punching you."

The other women laughed before noticing Olivia's silence. "Nothing is going on now. She said it was a mistake. Below average sex."

"Didn't sound below average to me," Sophie opined. "Unless she's a great actress."

"Pity sex, was what she called it. She took pity on a blubbering bitch. *Fuck.* I can't stop hearing her voice in my head."

"I'm so sorry, Liv." Cathy patted her on the arm as best she could.

"Oh, and my parents hate me, which I somehow find less painful than Keisha hating me. The cherry on top of my shit sundae is confusion about my sexual identity."

Sophie gazed down over the back of her seat. "These changes aren't easy, but you have a support system all around you. Ask for help and you'll get it. We're here for you, and the team has professional resources you can tap into. I didn't come out until I was nineteen. My parents were awful at first, but they came around eventually. I'm not saying your parents will, but give them time and space. Maybe they'll surprise you."

"Thanks, Cap."

"I'm not just your captain. I'm a friend, too."

"Thanks again. It's a lot to process. How do I even know if I'm gay?"

"It's different for everyone. Some people always know. Others know but deny it. Then there are the people who figure it out later. Maybe you're bi, or pan, or even ace, although ace seems unlikely given the amount of screaming I heard." Sophie grinned. "Don't be embarrassed. You had great sex. Be proud of yourself."

"It was really great. Mind-blowing."

"Has a guy ever made you scream so loud the people in the next room couldn't sleep?"

Olivia felt her cheeks coloring. "I'm really sorry about the noise, and no. Not even close."

"What about the emotional connection?"

"My brother asked me the same question. He's gay, by the way."

"I'd love to meet him. And? The connection?"

"I... I'm not sure."

"Emotional intimacy is a big part of it. Anyone can provide orgasms if they're skilled and determined, but only *you* can feel the emotional connection. Let me ask it another way. Did it feel right?"

"It didn't feel wrong, but then again, kissing a guy never felt wrong, either. I mean..." Olivia drifted back to her first kiss with Keisha at the strip club. She recalled the terror of discovery, but underneath her fear was something primal. An unshakeable imperative for more. The first kiss stalked the shadows of her psyche for weeks until she took a second sample last night. Olivia groaned as her memory served up their second kiss. Tentative, desperate, hopeful, and all too brief. She craved more, but once again let fear control her actions.

"It was the third kiss. My lips just melted into hers as if we no longer knew where I ended and she began. Our mouths burned, and I just wanted to be consumed in the inferno." An ocean of desire flooded Olivia's core as she gasped for breath. "Everything. Our kiss was everything."

"*Damn, girl.*" Cathy whistled.

"I know."

"Do you?" Svetlana asked. "Cap asked you if it felt right."

"Not just right. Perfection." Comprehension dawned, unbarring the gates of Olivia's mind. "Oh, damn."

I'm definitely not heterosexual, apparently... What to do about Keisha is a whole different question. I just wish I had a better answer than the one Keisha provided.

Olivia spent the flight lost in her thoughts. Turning her phone back on in Portland, she saw a text from Pat, asking for a phone call.

"Hi, Pat. You were right."

"I'm sorry, Livvy. How do you feel?"

"Strange. Keisha was horrible. She said terrible things, but I suspect she was trying to hurt me and wasn't completely honest. Or maybe I'm just hoping she wasn't."

"That's awful."

She mimicked a game show host's inflection. "*But wait, there's more.*" Inhaling deeply, she continued. "I'm a lesbian, or maybe bisexual. Not entirely sure. But I'm certain I like women, or at least one woman."

"Keisha, I presume?"

"Yeah," she sighed.

"Hang on." There was inaudible mumbling on the other end. "Bruce thinks you're crazy, but he is cheering for you. He's always had a soft spot for against all odds love stories."

"That's not what you told me about dating him."

"Oh, no, sweetie. I was easy. Incredibly easy." More mumbling. "Bruce says I'm a dirty tramp and should feel lucky he lowered his standards for me." Olivia giggled. "He's absolutely correct. I'm very grateful. *Anyway,* you're Bruce's chance for a glorious pageant of romance."

"Tell Bruce I'm sorry, but this tale is already dead on arrival."

"Hope springs eternal, my dear sister."

"Enough about me, Pat. I'm sure you didn't want to hear my sordid tales of misery."

"Of course I do, dear. However, I wanted to tell you I got a surprise call today. You'll *never* guess from whom."

"Mom and Dad?"

"Spoilsport." Pat didn't sound disappointed. "Got it in one, Livvy."

"Ugh. I'm sorry. What did they want?"

"Mmm, it was delicious, darling. They begged me—*begged*—to convince you to take Maxim back. I told them to fuck off, of course. Hush, Bruce." More mumbling. "Fine, first I told them to bugger off. Eventually they begged and pleaded so much I caved a tiny little bit."

She growled low in her throat, "*Pat.*"

"Here goes. Livvy, would you kindly consider taking back your philandering asshole of a fiancé to save our parents the gross indignity of facing the consequences of their own actions?"

She couldn't help but laugh. "When you put it in such a sweet and honest way, absolutely not."

Pat sniffed. "Well, I did my best."

"You're too much. You know that, right?"

"Bruce says the same thing. All the time," Pat said, his voice turning throaty and playful.

Her laughter rang out like pealing bells. "I love you so much, Pat. Today has been a complete shitshow, but somehow you managed to make me laugh."

"It's what I do, my love."

"Thank you. Did our parents have anything else to say?"

"What? Are you inquiring if they apologized for kicking me out of the family sixteen years ago? Absolutely not. In case you're wondering, they also didn't apologize for shoving all the expectations they had for me onto you at a vulnerable age. Because they're self-absorbed, insufferable assholes."

"Not surprising, though."

"Nope." He buried any resentment under ebullient cheer. "You and I turned out fantastic despite our parents' worst efforts."

"Thanks, Pat, although I partially disagree. *You* are an absolute treat. I'm still a dumpster fire."

"Even a dumpster fire provides warmth on cold nights, Livvy."

She choked. "Wow..."

"You are a good person, Olivia Kennedy. Bruce and I believe in you." She heard Bruce call out, "Believe in love, Olivia."

"I love you both. I'll come visit in the off season, I promise."

"We love you, too. Good night, Livvy."

"Night, Pat."

The ends of Olivia's lips twitched upward into the hint of a smile. *I can do this. Life, love, hockey. It'll all work out. Somehow.*

Chapter 18

Can't Get You Out Of My Head

Kylie Minogue

Once Keisha no longer had the distraction of film review, she couldn't block out the unquiet shadows lurking in the edges of her mind. *I could message Shelly for a hook up, but I can't just run to her bed every time an itch needs to be scratched. At some point it stops being fun and flirty—it becomes needy. Even worse, I'm not sure if seeing Shelly's blue hair between my legs is going to do it for me. Fuck. Every time I close my eyes, all I envision is blonde hair bobbing down below. I did the right thing. I know I did. She almost destroyed me and an "I'm sorry, Keisha" doesn't bring back a dozen years of my life. I keep telling myself the same thing over and over like I'm trying to convince myself. Cat says I should talk to someone, but I can't talk to anyone on the team. Definitely can't tell Mama. She would freak out.*

Keisha contemplated her next steps all the way home. *Actually, Mama might be the best person to talk to. She'll yell at me for being an idiot and set me straight.*

Keisha tossed her keys on the table and flopped onto the loveseat. She pulled out her phone and realized it was too late in Minneapolis to call. Levering herself back up, Keisha shuffled her way toward bed. Emotionally drained, she fell asleep half undressed.

Infernal beeping penetrated the thick fog of slumber before Keisha reached out a fumbling hand to slap her phone into blessed silence. She rolled over and sat up with a groan. Once done in the bathroom, she called her mother.

"Baby, it's early. Are you all right?"

"Hi, Mama. Not really."

"What's wrong?" The 'worried mom' tone was crystal clear.

"Nothing's wrong. I mean…I'm mostly good. I just made a mistake."

"What kind of mistake?"

Keisha drew air in deeply, steeling herself to say the next words. "I slept with Olivia Kennedy." She heard a gasp, then silence. "Mama, are you there?"

"I'm here, child. Not sure how much I wanna be after your bombshell, but I'm here. You best give me a minute."

She waited with a growing sense of dread for her mother to speak again.

"How drunk were you?"

"I was sober, Mama. It wasn't supposed to happen. She was in my room—"

"Why was she in your room?"

"Cat thought I would be out all night on a hook up, so she let Olivia in."

"All night hooking up in a strange city?" She heard the edge of disapproval in her mother's tone. "We'll need to have another discussion later. Go on."

Keisha groaned. *This conversation isn't going well.* She wiped a sweaty palm on her shirt before continuing. "She was in my room, dressed in a towel. We started yelling. I was about to punch her, and then she started bawling and saying how sorry she was. I didn't punch her. Then she kissed me. One thing just led to another from there."

"Uh-huh. Thank you for sparing me the details. I would ask what you were thinking, but clearly, you weren't."

"No, Mama."

"Are you going to sleep with her again?"

"Of course not, Mama."

"Then why are you calling me?"

"I..."

"*Shit.*" Keisha jumped. Her mother almost never swore. "You're calling me because you feel guilty about something else. Am I right?"

"Yes, Mama," she squeaked.

"Out with it."

"She came up to me yesterday morning, and I told her off. She looked...crushed. I feel a little guilty about how cruel I was."

"Why? Was what you said true?"

"Maybe a little bit. But I said what I said because I needed her to go away. It doesn't matter how incredible it was, we can never do it again. It was a huge mistake."

"I see." She waited for her mother to say more, sweat prickling her brow. Keisha opened her mouth to speak, then closed it when she heard her mother's soft voice. "Do you feel guilty for what you said to her, or guilty because you enjoyed sleeping with Olivia Kennedy?"

Keisha froze in shocked silence.

"You have some serious thinking to do, baby girl. I'm not sure I can help you sort this out."

"Mama, I won't sleep with her again, I promise."

Her mother's snort delivered another shock.

"Twice now you've sworn you won't sleep with her again. Who are you trying to convince? Me? Or you?"

"I..."

"Or did you want me to yell at you and tell you that you can't ever see her again?" Both ends of the line were still for a few moments before Tamika continued. "Oh, baby. Talk to me."

Keisha sniffled. "I liked it, Mama. Not just the...you know. For a moment, there was something different—better. You'll hate me, but for a brief instant, I never wanted it to stop."

"Why would I hate you?"

"Because it's *her*."

"I'm your mother, baby girl. I may not love all of your decisions, but I'll always love *you*."

"Thank you, Mama."

"Keisha, this is a bit much for me right now. I need to get ready for work. I love you very much and always have your back."

"Did I upset you?"

"Thinking about her is never easy, but no, you didn't upset me."

"All right, Mama. Thank you for talking."

"Thank you for calling, baby. I love you."

"Love you, too. I'll call you again soon."

Keisha sighed as she put her phone down. She cradled her face in her hands as uneasy thoughts ricocheted inside her skull.

I have more questions now than I did before. No, that's not true. I'm just considering issues I wasn't allowing myself to contemplate before. The most important being, do I want another taste?

Shaking her head to clear her thoughts, she chose to focus on getting ready for her volunteer work. Being a grant writer for a nonprofit was often a slog, but she was good at it and it made a difference. Crafting a mental to-do list required most of her brain power. Outside of a meeting with her director, she spent the morning asking companies and wealthy people for money to help address food insecurity. Keisha had a love/hate relationship with what she did—she loved helping people and hated how she lived in a society where many people went hungry on a regular basis. She went home after most of her volunteer shifts feeling like she helped people, although prolonged slumps in fundraising often pushed her toward depression.

Keisha went to practice after lunch. It was a disaster. The chemistry between her and Olivia was so bad Hicks called them into the locker room mid-practice to express her displeasure. When they didn't improve after being berated, she put them on windsprints until they puked. Exhausted and not fully able to wipe the taste of vomit out of her mouth, Keisha could only manage a meager whimper of protest when Hicks hauled her and Olivia into Caine's office.

"You need to do something," Hicks demanded.

"Hello to you, too, Coach. Why yes, I have been having a lovely day going over the billing from the New York trip. How about you?" Caine's eyebrows arched to match his sardonic tone.

"My day's been a fucking shitshow, thanks to these two imbeciles."

He steepled his fingers, voice suddenly frigid. "How may I help you?"

Hicks took a few breaths to settle herself. "Obviously, bringing Owens here was like throwing a match into a powder keg. I told you it was a horrible idea, but somehow it's worked. Until now."

Caine arched his eyebrows, waiting for their coach to make her point.

"Is couples therapy an option?"

Keisha and Olivia both exploded, "*We're not a couple.*"

Hicks rounded on them in fury. "That's not what half of the fucking hallway heard. I don't give a shit what your sleeping arrangements are. My *job* is to coach an expansion team full of draft picks, journeymen, and cast offs into a team capable of winning hockey games. It's been a dumpster fire from day one, and whatever weird on-ice chemistry you two have is one of the few bright spots.

But now you're absolute garbage, and I am not equipped to deal with your shit."

She whipped back to Caine. "I can coach them down there." She pointed in the direction of the rink. "But I'm not a psychologist—or psychiatrist—I don't know. Whoever handles this sort of crap." Inhaling deeply, she slowed down. "Sorry, I didn't mean to criticize mental health. I'm frustrated."

He tapped his finger on his chin, studying the chagrined skaters and their partially cooled coach. "We have a sports psychologist on the team, you know."

"I love Betsy to death, but this is well out of her wheelhouse."

"Fine. Let me see what I can do." He gazed at Hicks. "Coach, anything else for Kennedy and Owens?"

"No. You two are dismissed."

Keisha spun to leave, Olivia following directly behind her. "Coach, stay a minute," Caine said as Keisha opened the office door. She didn't look behind her as she stalked back to the locker room to change her clothes. Olivia was the only other person in the locker room, but Keisha studiously ignored her. In the shower, she focused on the tile in front of her. Unfortunately, keeping her eyes in one direction didn't stop her ears from hearing the water sluicing off the other woman's naked body. A supple body her subconscious mind seemed to delight in revisiting. She quickly finished her shower, nearly slipping on the slick tile in her haste. Keisha was dressed and walking to the door when she heard the water turn off.

She texted Cathy, asking to meet. Cat responded, directing her to a small bookstore about a mile east on Broadway. A short bus ride later, Keisha stepped into a cozy neighborhood shop conveniently named Broadway Books. The woman behind the counter wished her a pleasant afternoon as she entered. She spotted Cat browsing on the far side of the store.

"Hey, Cat—"

"*Shh*. The pink-haired woman's ears tried to match her hair color. Cat beckoned Keisha in close. "See the guy over there?"

Keisha peeked around the bookcase, spotting a bespectacled young man with an average build and a neatly trimmed beard shelving books. She spilled back, angling to face her friend. "The nerd?"

"Yeah...isn't he dreamy?"

She poked her head back to make sure, spotting no other guys in the store. Returning her gaze to Cat, she answered, "Not really my type."

"I am well aware. If you were into guys, though..."

"Probably still not, unless he's dynamite with his tongue." Cat's whole face went pink at Keisha's words. "What? I have standards."

"Keisha, you can't...do you think he's good with his tongue?"

"I have no idea." She eyed her blushing buddy. "Why don't you talk to him?"

Cat darkened from a rosy pink to a cherry red. "I asked for help finding a book a couple times."

"...And?"

"He found me one book, but of course I knew it was there before I asked. The second time, he special ordered a book for me. It was hot."

Keisha briefly pondered the vast gulf between their respective definitions of "hot." Shaking her head, she chose to focus on the immediate problem. "Have you tried asking him out?"

"No. I wouldn't know what to say."

She resisted the mounting urge to slap her own forehead with her palm. "Cat, you're a gorgeous, bad ass hockey player. He probably flogs his bishop on a nightly basis to women half as stunning as you. Just walk up and ask him out for coffee or something."

Cathy held up a hand. "First, gross. Second, you make it sound so easy."

Keisha ground her teeth before pitching her voice sweetly. "Do you think he's into you?"

"I'm pretty sure he checked out my bottom."

She stopped and took a moment to carefully observe her friend. Cat's black skirt was shorter than normal, and she eschewed her usual leggings for strategically ripped black stockings and Doc Martens. Her friend wore a white blouse with the top two buttons undone under a black and burgundy checkered sweater vest. Black eyeliner extended into small cat-eyes. "Holy shit, you dressed up for this guy."

Cat bobbed her head.

"Cat, I love you. Wait right here." Keisha wheeled and marched over to the young man. "Hi," she said brightly. "What's your name?"

"Mike," he answered tentatively.

"Hi, Mike. I'm Keisha. Can you help me?"

"Sure," he answered in a gruff tone.

"Right over here." Keisha reversed back around the romance books, waiting for him to follow.

"What are you looking for?" He asked in the same tone.

"Mike, this is Cathy. Cathy, this is Mike. Mike, do you have a girlfriend, boyfriend, or another type of significant other?"

"No, why?"

Keisha bulled onward, ignoring his queries. "Have you ever watched hockey?"

"A couple times at a friend's place."

"Perfect. Cathy here is a right wing for the Portland Blossoms. Go to the will-call window at 6 p.m. tomorrow night. There will be a ticket under Mike...what's your last name, Mike?"

"Graves. I—" The hapless bookseller had no chance to interrupt Keisha.

"Ticket under Mike Graves. Don't screw this up, Mike. Cathy likes you, and she'll be so pleased to see your face in the stands."

"Thanks, but what is happening..."

Keisha grabbed him by the shoulders and spun him back around, giving him a nudge as she said, "All right. Back to shelving books you go. I need to chat with my friend."

Mike meandered off with a dazed expression.

"Like he said, what just happened?" Cathy demanded.

Keisha wheeled back around to her friend. "If you score, then I will be credited for the assist." She grinned lecherously. Cat pouted back. "You like Mike. You're just all in your head about it. I merely helped."

Her friend folded her arms on her chest. "Thank you, but it's on me to ask him out, not you."

She wagged her finger in the air. "Which is why I didn't ask him out. I'm getting him to the game. The game where you will be on the ice. *You* have to take it from there." Her arms were suddenly filled by a giggling woman.

"You're right. Thank you again." She pulled away. "What if I'm still nervous? Or he doesn't like me?"

"Oh, sweetie. Once your nerd sees you skate, he's either going to be hooked on you, or he's going to be too intimidated to ever speak with you. Either way, you'll know if he's a good catch for you."

"I hope he's not intimidated."

She smiled. "Me too. Trust me. He will never find anyone better than you."

"Aw. You're sweet, Keisha."

"Not really. I'm sorry I haven't been a good friend lately. This whole Olivia thing has me off-balance." She paused. "What? Why are you smiling?"

Cathy looked positively giddy. "You said her name, and it didn't sound like a swear word."

"Don't make a big deal out of it," she grumped.

"Fine. Especially after practice today, I shouldn't read too much into it. Coach was *pissed* at you two."

Keisha's aching muscles needed no reminder. "Ugh. She suggested couples counseling for us. *Couples counseling.* I don't need to sit on a couch and talk about my feelings with that bitch."

Cathy's shoulders slumped. "And the moment is gone."

"Am I wrong?"

"Maybe. You and Olivia...your relationship wasn't healthy twenty years ago, and it was downright toxic *before* you did...sex stuff. I'm not even sure what's worse than toxic. Radioactive? Whatever it is, the two of you are not getting better. I feel awful saying this, but none of us expected anything good from having you both on the same team, but I think we all turned a blind eye to your problems when we started winning games."

The vein in Keisha's temple pulsed, pulling her skin taut with each accelerating heartbeat. She fought her instincts, and the seat of logic and reason commanded her diaphragm to draw in a deep, calming breath. The temptation to lash out dissipated enough to allow her to respond with calculated restraint. "Olivia—" The name tasted foul on her tongue. "—almost disabled me. I'm never forgiving her."

Her friend held her eyes, a melancholy smile playing on down-turned lips. "No one is asking you to forgive Olivia. Coach...and your friends...we want to help you *process*. Both of you."

"I appreciate the sentiment. I'm sorry again about shutting you out."

Cathy's smile dazzled. "You were having a rough patch. I'm so glad we're talking again." She slid her hand into Keisha's, dragging her to the other side of the bookcase. "What do you like to read? I *adore* romance books, but I'll read most things. Not true crime, though." She stuck out her tongue. "Blech."

"But you'll read mysteries?"

"Yeah. A mystery novel is fiction. Reading about actual people dying makes me sad."

"Makes sense." Keisha looked around the store. "I read sports books and biographies. History, too."

"No fiction?"

"Not since college."

Cathy pulled a book off the shelf, pressing it into Keisha's hands. "Try this one. For me." Those hazel orbs pleaded irresistibly. Keisha relaxed her hands to accept the novel. "Trust me, you'll like it."

"*Double Apex* by Josie Juniper? Formula One romance?"

"You like sports, you're smart, plus I've read this, and I loved it."

"Only for you, Cat. Are you getting anything, or do you just come here to ogle the staff?"

"*Hush.*" Her friend's voice rose into a squeaky whisper. "I buy books here. Just got distracted." Her eyes flicked over to Mike, gave him a deliberate once over, and returned to the bookshelf, accompanied by a subtle shiver. "He's dreamy," Cathy murmured.

"Pick something. There's a Thai place down the street that looks good, and I'm hungry."

Cathy's eyebrows raised. "No random hook up tonight?"

Keisha smiled. "I need a friend more."

Chapter 19

New Girl Now

Honeymoon Suite

Olivia banged the butt of her stick against the locker room floor before standing. She made her way to the ice with the rest of the team, soaking up the scattered cheers from the crowd. She nearly ran over Cathy, who came to a dead stop as they exited the hallway.

"*He's here. He's here,*" she exclaimed jubilantly.

"Who?"

Cathy jumped and waved toward the corner of the rink. A lone man wearing a Blossoms jersey stood, waved, and turned around to show her his back.

The right winger squeaked, hugging Keisha, Olivia, Dani and Heike, repeatedly gushing, "*He's wearing my number,*" before racing up ice to plaster herself against the glass.

Dani put on her most laconic drawl, asking, "Can someone fill me in?"

Keisha responded, "The nerd wearing Cat's number is Mike, her bookstore crush. She hasn't quite worked up the nerve to ask him out, but I made sure he got a ticket and her jersey."

"A jersey, too? No one gets a personalized jersey and a high-quality seat with a player will-call ticket." Dani observed.

"I told Caine I'd go to couples therapy with her." Olivia was surprised when Keisha jerked a thumb at her. "In exchange for a good seat and a named jersey for Cathy's crush."

Olivia shook her head, muttering, "Damn, I should have traded for something, too."

The two defenders chuckled at her comment before Heike jerked her chin in Cathy's direction. "She's got it bad, doesn't she?"

"Looks like it." Dani smirked.

The opposing team skated out for their warm-ups, forcing Cathy to skate back to her friends on the Blossoms side of the ice. The five of them began their stretching routines before skating around for passing and shooting drills.

As the team skated off the ice after warm-ups, Hicks pulled Olivia and her wingers aside. "Are your heads in the game today?"

As one, they answered, "Yes, Coach."

Hicks growled, "They fucking better be, or I will drop you back to fourth line so fast your heads will spin. I am *not* putting up with your shit." She pointed at Cathy. "Not you, Miller. You're a fucking angel."

They wisely kept silent.

"Dismissed."

Olivia reached out to tap Keisha on the shoulder as Hicks and Cathy walked off. "Hey."

The left wing scowled. "*What?*"

"Let's try and get Cathy a point in front of her guy."

Keisha's expression softened. "Agreed. Obviously don't waste a shot, but yeah. Let's get her some."

"Thank you for giving her the assist. You're very kind."

Olivia could see the condescending retort building behind Keisha's eyes, and then a rush of wordless breath. Finally Keisha said softly, "Cat's better than both of us. She's worth the effort."

"Yeah. She is." Olivia led the way to the locker room, her mind whirling. Those brief words marked the first civil exchange since their night together. *Is this a truce or just the lull before another storm? Maybe a bit of both. I don't deserve anything from her besides contempt, but I can't stop thinking of how her body felt pressed against mine, her nipple in my mouth, my fingers delving into her molten hot core.*

"Hey, bi—Olivia. You walked past the locker room."

"Sorry, I—" *Can't really tell you I was thinking of you naked and writhing. Shit. I need to get my mind on the game.*

Keisha glowered. "Do not screw up Cathy's night."

"I won't let her down."

Midway through the first period, Olivia got her chance. Keisha obliterated a Montréal skater in neutral ice, recovering the puck and tossing it into the offensive zone. Olivia rushed up ice, shouldering aside a defender to collect the disc. Rounding behind the net, she noted Keisha crashing the crease and Cat prowling the high slot. Feinting the wraparound, she passed to Cat, who whipped a wrist shot stickside for a goal. The goalie never saw the shot from behind Keisha's screen.

Sirens screamed, and the crowd roared. Cat pumped her fist as her teammates swarmed her under the flashing lights. She gave her guy a cheeky wave before grabbing one of Keisha and Olivia's hands in hers and lifting their combined arms into the air in a victory pose. Cat started chanting, "Kay Oh, Kay Oh, Kay Oh." The frenzied crowd read her lips on the jumbotron, and suddenly nine thousand voices rumbled the rafters, "Kay Oh, Kay Oh, Kay Oh."

Back on the bench, Hicks grunted. "Nice work, but we aren't done." Olivia could see a minute twitch at the corner of the coach's mouth crack her impassive façade. Early in the second period, Olivia fed the puck to Keisha, a perfect pass which she buried in the back of the net. Once again, Cat led an arena-shaking "Kay Oh" chant. Olivia soaked in the adulation and energy of the fans. She assisted Cathy on an empty net goal at the end of the game as the Blossoms defeated Montréal four to one.

Sitting adjacent to her linemate in the locker room, Olivia queried, "What's with the whole KO chant?"

Cat grinned from ear-to-ear. "Do you like it? You two have such amazing chemistry on the ice, and you deliver knockout blows."

"Too bad our chemistry off the ice is so bad." She noticed her friend's grimace. "I really like KO, though. We need something that incorporates *you*. In case you haven't noticed, you're a critical part of our line."

Cat leaned in to bump shoulders. "Aw, thank you." Olivia observed her friend's expression suddenly shift from playful to concerned. "Oh no. I need to find Mike. Do you think he'll wait for me? I think the showers are full."

"Shh. I'm sure he'll wait. He's an idiot if he doesn't and therefore wouldn't deserve you. Get ready, I'll take care of the shower situation." Two minutes later, Olivia barged into the showers, Cathy in tow. "Listen up, Cat here needs to meet a cute guy, so someone make some room."

Misty Thomas retorted, "Hasn't she already scored twice tonight? I guess she's going for the hat trick." The showers were filled with raucous laughter as Misty stepped back to allow Cathy to take her spot. "Go get him, girl," Misty said, smacking Cathy's butt as she passed.

Olivia lowered her voice to a volume barely above the ambient noise. "Thank you for giving up your spot."

Misty grinned. "I'm happy to help. Cathy's a sweetheart."

"Yeah." Her mind wandered as she waited for an open shower.

I haven't been open and friendly with my team this year, and I'm beginning to see how much of a mistake I've made. People will do anything for Cathy, yet I doubt they'd lift a finger for me. Since I'm no longer consumed with chasing Maxim's attention or whatever passed for affection from my parents, maybe it's time to do some self-improvement. Be a better friend, teammate, and overall person.

The next morning, Olivia stood at the front door of a local cat shelter at opening time. A smiling person with a shaved head and a plethora of tattoos unlocked the door and held it open for Olivia.

"Good morning."

"Good morning to you. Are you looking to adopt?"

"Actually, I'm hoping to volunteer."

"Do you have cats at home?"

"No, I live in a crappy studio apartment. I'm not sure it's suitable for human habitation, don't mention a cat."

They snorted. "I've lived in some of those. Next question. Have you worked with cats before?"

"No..."

"Ever had a cat at home?"

"No..."

"Can I ask why you're looking to volunteer with cats?"

Olivia realized she probably should have expected these questions. She couldn't think of a clever answer at the moment, so decided to try radical honesty. "I've been a miserable person most of my life. I want to be better, and I figure cats won't judge me."

The staff person cocked their head, mouth pursed in a slight frown. "I can honestly say I've never heard *that* answer before. When you say, 'miserable person,' can you provide more detail?"

"I've taken my friends for granted. When I was a teenager, I badly injured someone in a hockey game. I spent most of my life chasing validation from uncaring parents and pushed away everything good in my life. Um..."

"I was thinking more on the lines of animal, physical, mental, or substance abuse."

"Oh. None of those, unless being a terrible friend counts."

"You know what. Let me talk with Eileen, our volunteer coordinator. Why don't you take a look at the cats while you wait?" They pivoted and exited through a staff only door.

Olivia meandered over to the kennels and playrooms. The cats were mostly sleeping or grooming, but a few watched her. One in particular drew her attention. The cage card read Gorgon, age unknown. Inside was a black cat with one eye and a shredded ear. She pressed her hands against the cage, cooing at the feline. Gorgon stood up and stretched languidly before padding over. She licked Olivia's hands through the gaps, Olivia's heart melting with each swish of the sandpaper tongue.

"I don't know what happened to you, little girl, but you're still beautiful. Thank you for licking me. I'd love to play with you and scratch your little chin. You're so sweet. I can't get enough of you."

I've been careful about my expenses, but mental health is important as well, and I can tell right away that Gorgon and I are soulmates. Adopting this tiny companion is an expense I can justify.

Eventually, Olivia became aware they weren't alone. A stocky woman held out a hand, which Olivia shook. "Hi, I'm Eileen. I see you've met Gorgon."

"Olivia. Nice to meet you. Yes, Gorgon is a little purr machine. Do you know what happened to her?"

"We aren't sure. Possibly a coyote."

"Aw. She's a brave girl."

"She is. Um, can we talk?"

Olivia focused on Eileen. "Sorry."

She smiled. "I can't argue with someone who loves our cats. Which is obviously why you're here. Honestly, I was going to see you to the door, but watching you with Gorgon changed my mind. We can always use more people to clean cages, or give snacks or medicine."

"Of course, I would do anything asked of me."

"Good to know. First, can you tell me about yourself?"

"My name is Olivia...obviously, you know that. I'm a hockey player for the Portland Blossoms. I moved here last summer. My parents didn't allow pets growing up, so I was always jealous of friends who had them. I traveled around a lot, because...hockey player. This new league seems stable, and I'll hopefully be in Portland for a few years, at least."

Eileen bobbed her head. "I'm guessing a regular schedule will be difficult."

"Unfortunately, yes."

"We can work around your schedule. We'll probably have you pick up shifts here and there to cover for people when possible. I have some forms and releases for you."

"*Really?* Thank you," Olivia gushed. "Um. Do you think I could adopt Gorgon? I need to check my lease and buy supplies, but I think I might have found my new best friend."

Eileen's eyes crinkled as she laughed. "We'll put a hold on her for you. You'll have three days to get everything sorted out."

"Did you hear that, Gorgon? You and I might be roomies soon."

Chapter 20

Everybody Hurts

R.E.M.

Keisha inhaled the smell of car exhaust and rain before opening the door. She concentrated on keeping her pace deliberate and smooth, in contrast to the petulant stomp she desired. Her eyes quickly checked the building resident board before punching the up arrow to summon the elevator. She found Olivia sitting on a couch in the therapist's waiting area. Keisha took a seat in a chair, not bothering to acknowledge the other woman's presence.

"Good morning," Olivia said, her voice sounding far more cheerful than warranted for a Monday morning. Keisha grunted in response.

They sat in stony silence on separate couches, glaring at each other across a table covered with numerous resources for members of marginalized communities. Keisha picked at various pamphlets, thumbing through them to distract her attention from Olivia. She could sense the other woman squirming, and she feared Olivia was about to make conversation when a middle-aged person wearing a rainbow scarf and a sweater festooned with felines rounded the corner. Doctor Morgan introduced themself to Keisha and Olivia, who responded back before they followed the therapist to their office. Keisha eschewed the option of a couch, choosing a chair once again while Olivia seated herself on the couch.

Doctor Morgan sat facing them in another chair. "I'll start by suggesting some ground rules for our sessions. You may choose to agree or disagree to some or all of these rules, amend them, or add your own. It is important to establish consistent, mutually agreeable guidelines for our communication."

They spent some time establishing consensus before Doctor Morgan asked, "When did you two first meet?"

Olivia opened her mouth, but Keisha beat her to it. "About twenty-some years ago. My team was practicing before our first tournament. We were poor city kids in mismatched gear, and in struts this all-girls team in shiny, expensive gear with perfect matching uniforms. They played us for use of the ice and beat the snot out of us. That's when I first met the Puck Princess—I mean, Olivia."

"I don't remember that at all."

"Of course not. You treated us like gum on your shoe."

Doctor Morgan interrupted, "Ahem."

"Sorry. I *feel* like we were just a nuisance to you. I *feel* like you treated us as such."

"I'm sorry."

Keisha snorted. "I'm not. I started an all-girls team the next season and made it my personal goal to beat you. Being humiliated fueled me. Made me push myself to be better than you. And I proved it all, right before you almost killed me."

The therapist broke in. "Excuse me. What do you mean when you say Olivia almost killed you?"

"May I?" Olivia offered.

Keisha's blood was on fire, the urge to punch Olivia in her beautiful, perfect face as strong as ever. She wanted to ruin Olivia like Olivia nearly ruined her so long ago. Instead, she focused on her breathing and carefully, grudgingly uncurled her fists, placing her hands in her lap. She inclined her head and grunted permission.

In a soft voice, Olivia said, "Thank you. I first remember meeting Keisha about twenty years ago at a tournament. We knocked her team out in the first round, but her talent was already clear to me. My team won state championships in my first two years of high school. We were favorites to win a third in a row."

"Sorry, I need a drink." Olivia gestured at her water bottle before taking a long swig. "As the tournament went on, we started watching this team ranked near the very bottom. They shocked one of the top seeds in the first round and then just kept winning. I remember sitting in the stands, watching Keisha's team play. It was *her* team. The other players were decent. Some were good. Keisha, though...she was incredible. *Beautiful. Dominating.* An invincible force of nature."

Amidst the maelstrom of emotions churning in Keisha's guts, the tone of Olivia's recitation cut through the storm. She sounded soft and reverential, and Keisha wasn't sure how to react.

Olivia went on. "Her team wasn't good enough on their own to get out of the first round, but Keisha carried them on her back from victory to victory. I couldn't take my eyes off her. Whenever her skates touched the ice, I could feel the magic. I can't think of a better word. *Magic.* She made shots and passes like no one I'd ever seen. They were a Cinderella story by the time they made the quarterfinals and a sensation by the semifinals. Then it was us against them in the finals."

Keisha leaned back into her chair as she listened to Olivia's recounting of those fateful days. She'd never realized Olivia was in the stands watching. Her focus was always on the game in front of her. Keisha gripped the arms of her chair, knowing what came next. Her knuckles were bulging, and her fingers ached as they dug in.

"Our final game was back and forth. We scored first, then Keisha beat us short-handed to tie the game, then scored a go-ahead goal. We answered with two goals in the second period before she scored on a power play and later, a penalty shot. I remember trudging toward the locker room at the second intermission, totally exhausted. My father was standing outside the door. He grabbed my face mask and pulled me to the side. The only time I'd ever seen him so angry was when he'd kicked my brother out of our family for being gay. He screamed at me in the hallway. 'You look tired. You're playing like shit. How is one Black girl—well, he used another word for Black girl—beating you? I don't tolerate losers under my roof.' Then, he repeated something he'd told me and my brother for years, going back to his own playing days. 'If you can't win on the scoreboard, then you win by making the other motherfuckers bleed.' That's the kind of person my father was. Is."

Olivia looked over to Keisha, liquid shimmering in her eyes. "I'm so sorry, Keisha. I shouldn't have listened to him."

Keisha could only sit in silence.

"I scored the tying goal midway through the third period. On my next shift, Keisha checked me in the neutral zone, took the puck and was gone. She blazed past the defenders and beat the goalie on a breakaway while I watched from center ice. Her team held us off until the last few minutes when we pulled our goalie. We were doing everything to score a fifth goal to tie, and then I made a bad pass. Keisha scooped up the puck, deked a defender, and shot the puck down the ice. It was a perfect shot into an empty net for their sixth goal. It was my fault we lost. All I could hear in my head was my father's voice ordering me to make her bleed. I blind-sided Keisha into the boards at the bench. The crowd was so loud, I don't know if anyone but us heard her bones break, but I still hear the sound in my nightmares."

Olivia's voice trailed into a murmur. "I'm sorry, Keisha, for what I did to you. You should have been celebrating with your team, and I stole your moment from you. I took so much from you. You never deserved what I did, and no apology can ever make it right." She wept into her hands. They stared at her as she sobbed.

Doctor Morgan handed Olivia a box of tissues before turning to Keisha. "Can you talk about how you felt?"

"Angry. Very angry. No, 'angry' doesn't begin to cover what I felt. Enraged. *Enraged* is a great word. I relearned how to *walk*. The doctors said I would never skate again. Hockey was my life, and she robbed me of my life. I could have gone to the Olympics. *She* played in the Olympics and World Championships while I was trying to stay upright, both on the ice and in my wider life. I'm still enraged every time I think about it. How do I get over what she did? More importantly, why should I?"

"Those questions are why we're here."

"Not helpful, doc."

"Ahem."

"Sorry."

"Do you have anything to add to what Olivia said?"

"Yes, one thing. Before I passed out, I saw her snarling face looking down at me. There was so much hatred in her eyes."

Doctor Morgan asked, "What about now?" Olivia wiped her face, raising her head to meet Keisha's gaze. A shudder passed through her body as she choked out another sob. "What do you see today?"

"I..."

They spoke into the awkward silence. "Let's try a different question. Are you a different person today than you were ten years ago? Or twenty?"

"Of course."

"Why?"

"I've grown. Matured. I have a lot more experience and knowledge now."

"Think about how you've grown and matured over the next few days. I'll see you both again on Friday."

The walk from the office to the elevator was awkward, especially every time Olivia sniffled. Keisha avoided looking at her but couldn't help catching a glimpse of her red and misty eyes. Her glance was enough to initiate another round of blubbering, filling the elevator with sodden sniffles.

They exited into the gray, damp Portland day. Keisha tried to restrain herself from asking a question, but it ripped unbidden from her lungs. "How are you getting to practice?"

Another sniffle accompanied the answer. "I'm just going to walk."

"In this weather?"

Olivia's blonde head bobbed. "Yes."

"Come on. I'll walk with you."

"Really?"

"Don't make me regret it," Keisha grumbled. Four blocks later, the silence became too much. "Did you mean what you said earlier?"

Olivia swiveled her head toward Keisha. She looked less puffy and red. "Yes, but was there a particular part you're asking about?"

"When you watched me skate. You said I was beautiful."

"I'd never seen a more beautiful skater. You were magnificent. Every movement was precise, your passes were tape-to-tape, and your shot was a precision-guided missile. I was terrified, but I loved every moment I watched."

Keisha harrumphed. "Not anymore."

"No. You're so much better now."

"What do you mean?"

"Back then, you were incredible, but you were raw. Now, you understand the game on a much deeper level. Take Cat's first goal in the last game. You knew exactly where to be so when I came around and passed the puck, you were in perfect position for the screen. A dozen years ago, you were selfish because you had to be. Your team never would have won the final game without you. Today, you're unselfish and your game is elevated. Not only is your game better, but you make everyone else better. Again, last game on your goal...I didn't need to see you to know where you would be. Honestly, I could have passed the puck while blindfolded, trusting you would be in the perfect spot."

"Like on Cat's first goal of the season."

"Perfect example." Olivia stopped and touched Keisha's arm, slowing her to a halt. "Can I say something to you?"

"Sure," she grunted. "What is it?"

"I admire you even more now after our session today. After our first meeting, you made it your goal to be better than me, and you succeeded on every level. When you beat me, I could have done the same thing. I should have worked my ass off every day to be as good as you. Instead, I tried to bring you down. Of the infinite fuckups I have to apologize for, perhaps I have to apologize for my own weakness the most."

Keisha felt her blood pressure rising as Olivia continued. "I'm sorry. I wish I could change the past, but I can't. I can only control what I do now. You're still better than me, but now I'm pushing myself to be as good as you. Not as your rival, but as your teammate and partner."

She stared at the blonde's tear-streaked face, wanting to punch her again. Warring with her fisticuff desire was the urge to once again prove she was better by *not* punching Olivia. Keisha let her better nature win out. "I'm going to make you *work*, Princess."

Olivia grinned. "I would expect nothing less."

"Quit lollygagging and get a move on."

"*Lollygagging*?"

"What? Your Mama never told you to quit lollygagging?"

"No. She hired someone to scream at me in French." Olivia stuck her tongue out in disgust. "And my father hired someone to scream at me in Russian."

Keisha experienced a memory flash of Olivia's tongue caressing her pussy. She jolted into motion. "Come on, you can't beat me if we don't make it to practice."

<u>Chapter 21</u>

Opportunities (Let's Make Lots Of Money)
Pet Shop Boys

Twenty thousand voices howled as the two teams took the ice, Boston in green, Portland in pink. Forty minutes of scoreless hockey was in the books, only twenty minutes to go and the fans were about to blow the roof off. Boston typically played in a smaller venue, but tonight the men's basketball and hockey teams were not playing and the league scored the larger venue for a special game honoring women in Boston's history.

Olivia felt a rush skating in front of twice as many fans as normal. Clearly, Boston felt the same as both teams were playing frenetic, ferocious hockey. She bent low, focused on the puck drop to start the third. Her stick battled for control the instant the black disc bounced on the ice. Just over a minute later, she skated off the ice, lungs pumping like a bellows as the second line took over. She had about two minutes to recover her breath before her next shift. Boston dumped the puck, and both teams went for a change. Olivia, Keisha, and Cat mounted the boards, dropping onto the ice as each member of the third line entered the bench. Dani and Heike clambered onto the boards behind them as the defensive pair passed the puck to Keisha and went for their own change. Keisha slowed the pace, arcing through the defensive zone as Dani and Heike dropped into the rink and completed their change. Boston surged forward in an aggressive forecheck, chasing Keisha behind Svetlana's net. From there, she passed to Heike, and the Blossoms went on the attack.

Heike passed to Dani, who dumped the puck into the offensive zone. Olivia chased it into the far corner, wresting control and passing back to Heike, who cycled it to Dani, then Cathy, who reversed it back to Dani. Heike took the pass from Dani and shot wide of the net. Olivia's legs pumped as she collected the rebound, drawing two Boston skaters into the corner. The instant before she was sandwiched into the boards, she flicked the puck behind her to where she believed Keisha would be. Her teeth rattled and her aching lungs gasped desperately for breath, but the pain was worth it for the sweet sound of the goal siren.

The bench chanted "Kay Oh" as they skated over for celebratory fistbumps accompanied by twenty thousand boos. Hicks leaned down to ask, "How did you see Owens?"

"I didn't, coach. I just knew she'd be there."

"Are you fucking kidding me?"

Olivia exchanged grins with Keisha. "No, ma'am. Keisha's always where she needs to be. I just have to think of how to get her the biscuit."

"Call me ma'am again and you'll be doing wind sprints next practice."

"Sorry, coach."

Ten minutes later, Olivia found herself with the puck again, racing up ice toward the Boston net. Like a mongoose, she locked eyes with the netminder before flicking a look to the top shelf over the goalie's leather. Knowing the chasing defender would dive, she casually lofted a saucer pass to her left, never taking her eyes off the corner spot. Olivia's eye fake held the goalie's attention long enough for Keisha to collect the puck and bury it over the goalie's stick for her second goal.

This time, the crowd was quieter as they skated to the bench. Hicks leaned down again. "Another no look pass?"

"I could have done it blindfolded, coach."

Hicks snorted. "Don't say that too loudly. You know what they used to do to witches around here."

Olivia and her two linemates chuckled and exchanged grins. They were back on their feet a minute later to congratulate Misty, who scored an empty net goal to put Boston away for good. In the locker room after the game, Olivia walked over to Keisha, sitting next to Dani and Heike. Olivia asked the trio, "Any interest in a post-game celebratory dinner with me and Cat?"

Dani and Heike remained silent, waiting with their focus on Keisha. Olivia saw them visibly exhale when Keisha tipped her head, responding, "Yeah. I'll go." Dani and Heike quickly added their interest in joining. Once they were cleaned and dressed, Cat, Dani, Heike, Keisha, Olivia, and Svetlana stood outside the venue to discuss where to go.

"Irish pub," Cat suggested. "It is Boston, after all."

"Too touristy, especially around here," Svetlana countered.

Olivia was busy on her phone. "What about Italian? Looks like there are some good places nearby."

"Italian sounds perfect, but let's decide fast. It's colder than a moose's ballsack," Dani complained.

There were scattered chuckles as everyone agreed on the cuisine. Olivia steered them to a place five blocks away with a 4.8 rating on her map app. They all sighed in relief as the warm restaurant air enveloped them. Once seated, they discussed what to order, surprising the waitress with the sheer volume of food needed to satiate six hungry hockey players.

"Hey, Cat, what's up with your guy?" Olivia queried.

"It took some persuading, but we're having coffee on Friday."

"Persuading?"

"Mike's kinda introverted, I think. I like that about him."

"Among other things," Keisha teased.

"He's cute," Cathy retorted.

"Cat might not seem like it, but she's secretly a nerd."

"*Hey.* I mean...you're not wrong."

Keisha patted Cat's arm. "Your secret is safe with us."

Svetlana interjected, "Speaking of secrets. What is going on with those no look passes tonight? Did you two"—she pointed at Keisha and Olivia—"get abducted by aliens and have some kind of mind meld done?"

Olivia glanced hopefully at Keisha, but she seemed lost for words. "Keisha and I were talking after therapy on Monday. I said she was always in the perfect spot on the ice, so tonight I decided to test my hypothesis."

"So, you just blindly passed the puck, hoping she'd be there?"

"No. *Knowing* she'd be there."

"You're shitting me."

She snickered. "Hicks said the same thing. Well, with more expletives."

Dani eyed Keisha. "How did you know where to be?"

Keisha shrugged. "I just see the ice, and go where I think is best."

"You're fucking wild. You *putas* are crazy, but I love you."

Olivia giggled. "Thank you, I think." When no one said anything, she continued, "I have exciting news."

"What is it?" Cathy responded.

"Tomorrow, I'm getting a cat. Let me show you." Olivia opened her phone to the shelter website and found Gorgon's page. She passed the phone around to "oohs" and "ahhs" from everyone else. "I started volunteering at a cat shelter, and I met Gorgon. She's so sweet. Plus, black cats are statistically harder to adopt out because of superstitions."

Keisha snorted derisively. "Sounds about right." There were nods of commiseration and empathy around the table. "Sorry, go on."

"It's okay. Your point is valid. They think Gorgon might have been attacked by a coyote or another animal, which is how she lost her eye and part of her ear. She's very snuggly."

Cat asked, "What are you doing at the shelter?"

"Mostly I'm filling in for people who are out because my schedule is so fluid. If no shifts need to be covered, then I'll help with socializing."

"Your volunteer job is playing with cats?"

"It's more than just playing with cats. Playing helps keep their minds engaged and their hunting instincts strong. It also helps them bond with their humans so they're more likely to be adopted and have successful outcomes."

"Huh. So, playing with cats," Heike teased, the often taciturn German's face splitting into a broad grin. "Seriously, Gorgon is cute, and you're doing a good thing. Will you keep her name?"

"I think so. I like it."

The rest of the table traded pet stories until dinner came. Everyone enthusiastically dug into the heaping platters of steaming pasta. They shared around the table, trading tortellini for linguine before lapsing into silence punctuated by giddy, food-loving moans. Olivia finished up her meal by sopping her bread into the buttery garlic sauce of her scampi, savoring each floury delivery of flavor. Finally full, she leaned back and observed her teammates as they each concluded their meal. *Being social with my team is pleasant. Enjoyable, even.*

Olivia addressed the table. "Hey, everyone. Thank you so much for coming out to dinner. I know I've been an icy bitch most of the season. There's a ton of abysmal reasons for my actions, but they aren't important now. I appreciate the second chance and pledge to be better."

They all looked at her, seemingly unsure what to say. Svetlana cracked a smile, inclining her head toward Dani. "Since we're in an appreciative mood, thank you for introducing me to your brother. I can't wait to get him back in bed."

"*Oh my God.* You're so gross, Lana. Please don't talk about sex with my brother." Dani's whole body shuddered. "I just ate." Everyone except Dani laughed. The mirth continued as the six of them made their way back to the hotel.

The team flew back to Portland the next day, arriving just in time for Olivia to pick up Gorgon and take her home. Gorgon explored the apartment tentatively, poking her head into the litter box before hopping onto the bed and curling up on a pillow. The onyx feline got up when Olivia fed her, but quickly returned to her spot.

She found herself face to face with Gorgon when she went to bed, the cat's slightly fishy breath in her nostrils. "Good night, little lady. Welcome to your new home. It's not much, but it's ours." Gorgon unhurriedly blinked her one eye and stretched out, exposing her tantalizingly soft belly. Olivia knew not to fall for the tummy trap. They drifted off to sleep together.

Olivia socialized cats in the morning before her appointment with Keisha at Doctor Morgan's office. This time, Keisha chose to sit on the couch with her. Olivia took this as a sign of progress.

The therapist started the session by catching up with them on how they were each doing before asking, "At the close of our first session, I asked you to reflect on how you've grown and matured. Would either of you care to share?"

Keisha spoke first. "Given my...situation after the injury, I was forced to undergo a significant change in my lifestyle. The determination I previously felt to improve myself became a drive to recover so I could one day get revenge."

Olivia shivered, remembering the beating on Keisha's first day and wondering what more might be in store.

"Revenge is a negative goal, and my Mama helped me find a more positive purpose. I spent time with my team, training and mentoring them. If I couldn't help by playing, then I wanted to help by improving their game. In college, I assisted the coaches. Over time, I became less focused on what I wanted and more concerned about helping others. After college, I started working at a non-profit to assist people experiencing food insecurity. Even now, I've been told by someone"—she nodded at Olivia—"my play in the rink is more selfless than it was before."

Keisha punctuated her last sentence with another glance at Olivia.

"Olivia, do you have any reaction to what Keisha shared?"

She angled her body to semi-face Keisha on the couch. "Keisha, I am constantly in awe of your bravery and determination. You've come back from an injury that would have broken many people. I understand your desire for revenge because I fully deserve it." She rubbed her damp, sweating palms on her leggings. "Your drive to help hungry people is admirable. You're one of the kindest people I know. I mean, not as kind as Cathy, but she's an angel."

Keisha chuckled, nodding her head in agreement.

"You inspire me. Every time you've encountered an obstacle in your life, you've risen above it. I want to learn from you how to do the same."

Chapter 22

Revelation (Mother Earth)

Ozzy Osbourne

Olivia fucking Kennedy is inspired *by me? Is this some kind of weird ploy to get on my good side, or is she genuinely honest? I'm not sure what to make of this.*

"Keisha? Keisha? Are you still with us?"

"Oh, sorry, doc. I was processing."

"Anything to add?"

"I appreciate Olivia finding me inspirational."

"Good. Perhaps you could say it to Olivia rather than me."

Keisha adjusted her position to be closer to facing Olivia. She straightened her spine and inhaled deeply. "Olivia, I am grateful you find me to be kind and inspirational. I'm delighted to hear your words."

The other woman bowed her head. "Thank you," she murmured.

"Olivia, would you care to reflect on how you've grown and matured?"

"Of course." They kept a silent vigil while Olivia composed her thoughts. "It's hard to know where to start. I guess I'll start around the time when we first met, even if I didn't realize it at the time. Growing up, I always felt like an afterthought. Patrick, my brother, was the golden child. Smart, outgoing, incredibly good at hockey. My parents doted on him, and I hated him for it. They constantly showered him with attention and praise, although sprinkled with a heavy dose of criticism. Meanwhile, I always felt as if I wasn't enough, largely because I was a girl. Publicly, things were different. Everyone called me the Puck Princess, a name I hated at first but later embraced. Patrick, though—he was destined to be king."

Olivia paused for a sip of water. "Everything changed when I was fourteen. Pat was in college when one of his teammates walked in on him having sex with another guy. My parents were outraged, but mostly they were desperate to contain the scandal. Then Pat decided he was done hiding who he is. He came out as gay, quit hockey, and became an art major."

She chuckled wryly. "He knew exactly how to push Dad's buttons. The three things Dad hated most could pretty much be summed up as gays, quitters, and artists. Sorry, Dad hated four things. Pat started dating a Black guy."

Keisha's gaze met Olivia's and she witnessed the small, weary shrug of her teammate's shoulders at her father's racism.

"My parents disowned him. They literally cut him out of family photographs. Suddenly, I was no longer an afterthought. *All* of my parents' demands and expectations came down on me. If Pat wasn't going to be the next king of hockey, then I was to be the queen. I don't know how he bore their pressure for so long. No pass was clean enough. No shot was accurate enough. No check was hard enough."

Olivia's hands were balled into fists in her lap, and her voice cracked. "*Nothing. Was. Ever. Enough.* More than anything, *I* was never enough. No matter what I did, I could never be as perfect as Pat had been. I tried. I tried so hard to be perfect, but even if I could have been, it still wouldn't have been enough because I wasn't a man."

Olivia paused to wipe away the salty tears brimming on her eyelids. "Then along comes Keisha and her magical run to the championship."

She looked Keisha directly in the eye. "I wanted to be you so much. Your mom was cheering for you, supporting you, *loving you*, in ways my parents never did. And your game...I'd watched you play, but seeing you isn't the same as *playing* against you. Your energy. Your *joy*. I was overjoyed to witness greatness firsthand. At the same time, I was transcendently jealous. When you scored the empty netter to finish us off...I lost my mind. Not only was I not good enough to be Pat, I wasn't remotely good enough to be you. None of this is an excuse for what I did. There was and never will be a justification. I could never be you, so I hurt you instead. What I did was... unconscionable. With all of my heart, I wish I could take it back. I'm so sorry."

The waterworks resumed as tears fountained from Olivia's eyes, running unchecked down her cheeks. Keisha surprised herself by scooting over on the couch to let Olivia slump against her chest. Rivulets of warm tears dampened her shirt as Olivia bawled in Keisha's arms. *Apparently Olivia's tears are my kryptonite. This is the second time I've held her as she cried like a baby. On the plus side, I won't sleep with her this time.*

Olivia eventually composed herself and sat upright again. "You asked me how I've matured and grown over the years. The honest answer is I didn't. I kept chasing my parents' expectations, but I slowly started to give up. I missed the last Olympics because I wasn't playing well enough to justify making the roster. I've been going through the motions for years now. In hockey. In my life. I was engaged to a man I didn't love, and who cheated on me constantly, because my parents wanted it. I played just well enough to not get cut because I'm too afraid to find out what my life would be without hockey."

She raised her head to meet Keisha's gaze. "Then Keisha comes along and everything changes. Sure, she beat the shit out of me, but I deserved it. I've rediscovered my love of hockey again. I'm not engaged to a worthless shithead anymore. I cut my parents out of my life, although they cut me out as well. We—" Her ears, cheeks, and neck flushed a brilliant pink. "I'm exploring new sides to my sexuality. I started volunteering." Olivia's eyebrows shifted down and she pursed her lips. "Keisha, when I said you inspire me, I mean it. Regardless of what happens with therapy, or the team, or life in general, you've shown me a better way to live, and I'm embracing a new direction."

Keisha stared at Olivia until the therapist asked, "Keisha, do you have any reaction to what Olivia shared?"

"Yeah. That is some fucked up shit. Sorry, doc."

She could hear the smile in Doctor Morgan's voice when they responded, "Perhaps you'd like to provide some clarifying detail to your answer."

"Give me a minute. Please." She reviewed everything she heard Olivia say and pondered how to respond. "First, thank you for sharing. Second, your parents seem like assholes. Well, I'm not sure about your mom, but your dad sounds like a monster. I can see why you—" Keisha rolled her shoulders back to loosen up and quickly shook her head.

"Sorry. I was about to say something judgemental. I *heard* you say your early life was in the shadow of your brother. You felt neglected and unappreciated. Kudos to your brother for coming out and living his truth regardless of your parents' disapproval. It's unfortunate your parents placed such unrealistic expectations on you in his absence."

Keisha felt her heart rate increase and her skin went clammy. Beads of sweat popped on her brow and armpits. "I understand why you blindsided me. What you did was not okay. It was a dirty hit, and I'm not sure..." Her stomach clenched alongside her fists. Her mind raced back to her memories of the searing agony followed by the foggy confusion of waking up in the hospital. "I'm saying it makes more sense as to what was going through your head. I just..."

She leapt up, slamming a fist into an open palm. Whirling around, she paced frantically. Back and forth until she stopped, knuckles gripping the back of the couch so hard it hurt. "I *hate* you, Olivia. I've hated you for over half my life. You stole my goddamn future from me when I was barely seventeen. Even worse, you had the golden opportunity to do everything you made sure I couldn't, and you *fucking wasted it.*"

Olivia sat tall, absorbing Keisha's withering diatribe with the barest of flinches.

Keisha slumped, whispering, "You tell me I inspire you, but how can I inspire anyone when I'm filled with so much hate?"

The blonde woman cautiously reached out a hand, placing it over Keisha's and gently squeezing.

"I'm tired of it, Olivia. I'm tired of being angry. I'm tired of hating you. Of letting negative energy dominate my life. I'm just exhausted. I need to stop." She whirled around and grabbed her coat as she ran for the door. Eschewing the elevator, Keisha flew down the steps and out into the cold and wet Portland air. The day perfectly matched her mood. Spinning to face the river, she jogged across a nearby bridge, frigid air savaging her lungs. She crossed the bridge and walked through the Riverfront Park. Keisha held her arms tightly around her ribs as wintry tendrils of air sought gaps in her coat. She watched the Willamette stoically flow by, heedless of her internal turmoil.

I thought I needed to be alone, but I was wrong. Loneliness sucks.

A bridge up ahead crossed back over the river right near the arena. She was late for practice, but she didn't have to be too late, and luckily practice was here today. Flexing her toes to keep blood flow going, she hustled across the Steel Bridge. The locker room was empty when she arrived. Gearing up, she tottered toward the ice.

Hicks cocked an eyebrow. "Kennedy said you weren't feeling well and wouldn't make it. Was she lying?"

"No, coach. It was a tough session today. I don't want to talk about it. Suffice it to say I'd rather be here with the team than alone. It just took some walking to figure it out."

The coach nodded. "Don't make a habit of it. Stretch out and join practice."

Cat and Olivia skated over as Keisha was warming up.

Concern was written all over her pink-haired friend's expression. "Are you okay? You never miss practice."

"Olivia didn't tell you…"

"No, Liv only said something to Hicks."

"Yeah. I'm all right, Cat. Can you give me and Liv a moment alone?"

Olivia's lips curled upward as Cathy skated away. "Liv? That's new."

"Just trying it out. Thanks for not telling anyone."

"Of course. What happens during the session stays there. Are you really all right?"

"Maybe." Keisha meant to say something about the session, but "Do you want to have dinner with me tonight?" came tumbling out of her mouth instead.

They stood staring at each other, dumbfounded. Before Keisha could take it back, Olivia whispered, "I'd love to have dinner with you tonight. I just need to feed Gorgon first."

"Right. You've got to feed the cat." There was an awkward pause as she fought for something else to say. "We can talk after practice."

"Perfect." Olivia's grin was perfect as well. She even winked before she skated off.

Keisha stood at center ice, admiring Olivia's ass as she rejoined practice. *Did I just ask Olivia fucking Kennedy out on a date?*

Chapter 23

Lunch

Billie Eilish

I think Keisha Owens just asked me out on a date. Is this real? What am I going to wear? I felt like today's session went well, but this is crazy, right?

Someone rapped her lightly on the shoulder with a hockey stick. "Wuh?"

"Hey, Kennedy? Where's your head at?"

"Oh. Sorry, Misty." Olivia turned her attention back to faceoff drills. They were both hovering just below fifty percent for faceoff wins this season, and Hicks wanted them to push for fifty-five or sixty percent. She adjusted her grip on her stick and anticipated the puck drop.

Hicks called Keisha and Olivia over at the end of practice. "Is there anything I need to know?" She quickly raised her hand to forestall a response. "Let me rephrase the question. Do I need to worry about the two of you?"

They chorused, "No, coach."

"Good. Make sure you keep your shit together. We might even make the playoffs, so I don't need to worry about Toronto *and* the two of you."

"Yes, coach."

Olivia settled on the locker room bench next to Cathy. "You're going out with Mike tonight, right?"

"*Yes.* I'm still trying to decide where to take him. Should we go clubbing?"

"As in dancing? Has he expressed any interest in clubbing?"

"No, but..."

"What kind of music does he like?"

"We haven't talked about music yet." Cathy was suddenly looking skittish.

Olivia laid a calming hand on her friend's arm. "Maybe see if there's a pub trivia night you can go to."

"Liv, I love it," Cathy squealed. "What about you? Date night with Gorgon?"

Olivia's eyes flicked over to where Keisha was stripping off her equipment.

Her friend must have noted the glance because she gasped, "*Noo. Shut the front door.*"

"What?"

Cathy leaned in to whisper, "Are you going out with Keisha?"

Olivia deflected. "Why would you think we're going on a date?"

"Because you ogled her briefly and you had this teeny-tiny ghost of a smile. Also, you said 'date,' not me. You *like* her. Does she like you?"

"I'm not sure...it's complicated."

Cathy darted across the room in a flash of pink hair and matching pink practice jersey, whispering and gesturing with Keisha. Olivia could see her teammates around the room following the commotion.

Cathy, please don't mess this up for me.

Her friend sauntered back to retake her seat. "She asked you on a date. You're going on a *date.*" Cathy paused for dramatic—and triumphant—effect. "*Together.*"

Olivia could feel every eye in the room on her as blood heated her cheeks and ears. "That's how dates work," she hissed. "Two people, together." Cathy quivered, grinning with a gleam of euphoria in her eye. Olivia added sarcastically, "And could you talk a bit louder? I don't think they heard you in the showers."

"You're right." Cathy stripped off the rest of her clothing and skipped into the showers. Olivia followed a minute later at a more sedate pace. Dani and Heike's twin curved eyebrows were impossible to miss. Heike stuck her head under Olivia's shower head to whisper, "I'm rooting for the two of you. If you score together, who gets the assist?" The big defender's grin was toothy as she spun toward the exit.

Well, at least our teammates are supportive.

Olivia turned off her shower when she was done, trying not to stare at Keisha, who was the only other person left in the showers.

She heard Keisha's shower turn off as she was leaving, and added a bit of extra sway to her hips, just in case the other woman was watching.

The last of the other players trickled out, leaving them alone in the locker room. Keisha stood and dropped her towel. Her head twisted at Olivia's inadvertent gasp. Her gaze and voice held a challenge as she said, "Come on. I've already seen it all anyway."

Olivia's knees quivered as she levered herself upright. She felt her skin flush as she fumbled with the knot holding her towel together. The knot released and her towel fell to the floor, accompanied by a low whistle. "Not bad, Liv. Not bad at all."

She raised her eyes to drink in Keisha's athletic form. "You, too, KO."

"I thought we were KO together."

"On the ice, yeah. Off ice and undressed, you're definitely a knockout."

Keisha grinned. "Then call me Knockout. Let's leave KO as our thing out there." She inclined her head toward the rink.

"Cat's going to be so disappointed I have a nickname for you before she does."

She chuckled. "Honestly, I can't believe she never came up with it. Now get dressed and let's go feed Gorgon."

"You're coming to my place?"

"So long as you don't mind."

"I'm going to warn you, I have a shitty studio apartment."

Keisha shrugged. "Same. I'm going to look for a slightly bigger place in the off season."

"I hate my current place, but I'll probably keep it. The rent is affordable, and as I'm sure you're aware, my finances are a mess."

"I know. You ready?"

"Yeah. Let me grab my coat."

They were almost at the door when Hicks' voice brought them to a halt. "Don't go anywhere, you two." They wheeled simultaneously.

Olivia asked, "Are we in trouble, coach?"

"Should you be?" Hicks' face beamed, and she belly laughed. "I'm not sure why you both look guilty, but I'm glad you're not clawing each other's face off, so I won't ask questions."

Keisha put her hands on her hips. "What can we do for you, coach?"

"I just got off the phone. You two are on the bubble for the national team."

"*No shit,*" they squealed simultaneously. Both quivered with excitement.

"Miller's close. If you three play in March like you've been playing these past few months, then I'm pretty sure you'll punch your ticket to Oslo. I'll talk to Caine about making sure you've got everything squared away for transatlantic travel."

"Thank you, coach," they chorused.

"You're welcome. Now, go have a good night. I'll tell Miller tomorrow."

"Night, coach."

They waited until they closed the door behind themselves to break into a fit of dancing, giddy squeals, and finally a hug. "Is this weird?" Olivia asked.

"Hugging or possibly going to the World Championships?"

"Both, but mostly hugging."

Keisha sighed into her hair. "It's a bit weird, but I like it so far."

"Me too," Olivia murmured.

She felt Keisha nudge her ribs, breaking the moment. "Okay, once we talked about it, it got too weird. Let's go feed your cat and figure out dinner."

"Right. Do you have a car?"

"Nope. You?"

"No. I usually take the bus."

"Bus works for me."

Olivia's heart raced faster when Keisha chose to sit next to her on the bus. She could feel the other woman's warmth where their legs rubbed together. They swayed and jostled as the bus lumbered through the streets of Portland. Each of them pulled out a book to read, although Olivia struggled to focus on the pages. Instead, she savored every opportunity for her body to rub against Keisha's. She regretfully pulled the chain at her stop, bringing their quiet reverie to an end.

After a short walk from the bus stop, Olivia opened the door to let Keisha into her apartment. "I'm sorry about this place."

"Don't sweat it. I've seen worse. *And holy shit.*" Keisha wandered over to the two garment racks laden with clothing. "No wonder you had to do porn." She whirled to face Olivia, eyes wide and her hand clapped to her mouth.

Olivia fought down an angry retort. She felt the hot flush in her cheeks and ears as she responded with meticulous neutrality. "Keeping up my image was stupidly expensive, but I'd hoped the payoff of marrying Maxim's wallet would be worth it. Mostly for my parents' sake, but a little for me. His dick certainly wasn't worth the effort." She sighed. "I'm such an idiot."

"You're not an idiot. You just made some bad decisions because you felt they were better than the worse decisions."

"Thanks, Keisha. If you want any of those, help yourself."

"Oh, girl. Don't tempt me with a good time." Keisha spun back to the garment racks. "Speaking of...what are you wearing tonight?"

"I hadn't given it much thought." *Unless you count almost every minute since you asked me out, then yes, I've thought of almost nothing else besides what I would wear, what you would wear, how your lips taste or what your skin feels like under my fingertips,* Olivia thought.

"May I try some on? I think some of these might fit me."

"Yes, of course. Try on anything you like."

Olivia ducked down to peer under the bed. "Hi, sweetie. It's okay. Why don't you come out to meet Miss Keisha? I think you'll like her." With more cooing and a few treats, she managed to coax Gorgon out from under the bed. *"Good girl. Brave girl.* Why don't you—" Olivia's throat tightened up at the vision of Keisha, clad only in her underwear, casually browsing the garment rack. Gorgon, unperturbed by a scantily-clad human, courageously trotted over to rub herself against Keisha's ankles. Olivia gulped audibly when the other woman dropped into a squat to pet the cat, her panties tight against her rump.

Any hopes about her reaction being unheard were dashed when Keisha glanced over her shoulder, a wicked grin on her face. Keisha ratcheted up the tension by subtly twerking as she petted the cat. The gusset of Olivia's underwear quickly moistened.

"Your cat is adorable. I think she likes me."

"Thank you. She hasn't met many people."

"Who takes care of her during away games?"

"One of the other shelter volunteers is a Blossoms fan. She has a daughter in Girl Scouts, and she offered to look after Gorgon while I was away on road trips in exchange for me chaperoning two weeks of Girl Scout Camp this summer."

Keisha's shoulders shook with laughter. "Oh no. I'm just imagining you living in a tent for two weeks."

Olivia felt her blood run cold. "A tent? I thought it would be cabins or something semi-civilized."

The other woman patted her knee. "You might want to check to be sure what you got yourself into."

"Yeah. You're right." She shook her head, standing and walking to the kitchen with a pause to retrieve Gorgon's bowls. The cat's attention was fully focused on Olivia the moment she heard a can open. Gorgon planted herself by Olivia's feet, patiently waiting for the chalice of deliciousness to descend. Olivia refilled the water bowl and placed it back in its spot.

Keisha was pulling on an eggshell white minidress that dipped low in the back when Olivia looked up. "Zip me up?"

Olivia could only nod, her tongue stubbornly refusing to function. Her brain was in no position to complain as synapses fired at a glacially slow pace. Fingers fumbled with the zipper, miraculously not tearing the fabric as she pulled it up.

"What do you think?" Keisha giggled as she pirouetted.

"*Fucking hell,*" Olivia whimpered.

Keisha lifted her heels off the ground, balancing on the balls of her feet. "Imagine how this would look with stilettos," she teased.

Olivia ran her eyes up Keisha's elongated calves and taut thighs to her ass, which popped even more due to the pose she held. She desperately wanted to retrace the journey her eyes made with her tongue. Olivia shivered as her pussy gushed.

"What's wrong? Cat got your tongue?"

"You're killing me, Knockout."

Somehow Keisha's grin grew larger. "Too bad about the heels."

"What size are you?"

"Nine and a half or ten, depending."

"I wear a size nine or nine and a half. I bet some of my shoes will fit you. Want to check and see?"

"*Heck yeah.*"

Olivia led her over the bed and slid a box full of shoes from underneath. "I'm pretty sure I've got something courtesy of years of retail therapy. Which, I have to stop calling it that. Yet another thing I'm working on, because shopping to make myself feel better is how I got myself into financial hell. Anyway, take a look." She slid out another box of shoes next to the first. "I'll find something to wear for myself." Olivia shed her clothes as she strutted to the garment racks.

A furtive glance confirmed Keisha's focus on her ass. *"Two can play this game,"* Olivia thought as a subtle smile graced her lips.

Browsing through her clothing, she was tempted to go with a black dress. The contrast with Keisha would be stunning. She eschewed temptation, opting for an emerald off-one shoulder dress which better matched her mood. Slipping into the dress, she glanced up to catch Keisha observing every movement, a pair of strappy white sandals hanging limply in her fingers.

She sauntered back to the bed before whipping around. Flashing a coquettish grin over her shoulder, Olivia teased. "Zip me up?" Keisha dropped the sandals on the bed and tugged the zipper upward. "Where are we going for dinner?"

Keisha pondered the question for a minute. "Originally, I was planning on a local food pod with warm and covered shelters, which would have been perfect for sweatpants and hoodies. Now, we need a new plan. There's a brewpub on Broadway near where Cathy's crush works. I think it used to be a church. Sound good to you?"

"I've been past it a few times and always wanted to try it, so this is perfect."

"How do you feel about a Lyft or a cab?"

"Works for me. How about one of us gets the ride there and the other gets back?"

"Perfect. I'll start."

Olivia took a deep, calming breath when she realized she'd just asked Keisha to come back to her apartment after dinner. *She'll just change clothes and leave. I don't have to make a big deal over it. I'm sure she won't want to spend the night. Do I want her to spend the night? Yes. I definitely want her in my bed. But only if she wants it, too. Just breathe. Put on your heels. Your sexy heels to go with your sexy dress for a date with a beautiful woman in an equally sexy dress and heels. This isn't helping my anxiety.* She grabbed a wand toy to play with Gorgon, entertaining all three of them while they waited as she tried desperately not to think of what she and Keisha could do with a completely different kind of wand toy.

She fidgeted the entire ride to the restaurant. Her hand wanted to seek out Keisha's, but there was just enough space between them to make any contact seem obviously contrived. Even so, her hand meandered about midway between them. Olivia twitched in her seat when she felt Keisha's pinky finger graze her own. They each stared studiously forward as Keisha's little finger subtly caressed Olivia's. Her pinky finger moved in response, slowly tangoing with Keisha's. They both seemed reluctant to acknowledge the forbidden dance their smallest fingers were engaging in.

Arriving at the restaurant broke the spell. They climbed out of their respective sides, hurrying through the drizzling darkness to find refuge, warmth, and refreshment inside. Taking seats on opposite sides of a small table, they perused the menu and placed an order with the waitress. Once their order was done, they both settled back in their chairs to wait. The silence transformed from pleasant to awkward until Olivia couldn't take it anymore.

"I'm sorry. I feel the overwhelming urge to acknowledge how strange this is."

Keisha responded with a toothy grin and wry chuckle. "You're telling me. I've hated you for almost as long as I can remember, and now we're sitting across from each other, on a *date,* wearing fancy clothes—*your* fancy clothes. This feels surreal."

Olivia studied the grain of the wood on the table, unable to look up. "Do you still hate me?"

She heard Keisha's bellows-like exhalation. "I don't know anymore." Keisha's fingers tapped absently on the table. "Hate is almost a habit at this point. Like a comfortable old sweater. Then again, it was so easy to hate you when I didn't actually *know* you. Now, though..."

Olivia dared to look up when Keisha paused, finding those glittering brown eyes staring at her. She didn't look angry. More like the expression of someone stuck on a master-level sudoku. Olivia wanted to reach across the table, but her arms weren't responding.

Keisha continued, "I still *want* to hate you, because it's familiar. I know we're not supposed to talk about our sessions outside of therapy, but today gave me a glimpse into the shitshow of your life. Not only am I tired of being so angry, it's so much harder to be angry at you when I understand more about who you are as a person."

Her arms finally decided to move, allowing her hands to slide across the table where Keisha tentatively placed her own hands into Olivia's.

"One more thing. Talking about my feelings helps. I guess I see it like this. I hate the Puck Princess and probably always will. Olivia Kennedy, on the other hand, I—" Keisha made an "L" sound, then shut her mouth and shook her head fiercely, her tight curls bouncing and swaying. "I like Olivia Kennedy. Am I making any kind of sense?"

"Yes. I am the Puck Princess, though." She shrugged. "I am and I'm not."

Keisha squeezed her hands. "It's complicated." She added her own shrug. "Life is complicated. Let's just keep talking and see what happens."

Olivia's eyes flicked to their hands. "I like what's happening so far."

They both grinned. Their moment was interrupted by the arrival of beer.

The server held out a glass and said, "One IPA." Olivia raised her hand.

"And you must be the pilsner. Your food will be out shortly."

"Thank you."

Olivia took a sip of her beer. "Mmm. This is good. Their strawberry basil margarita was almost irresistibly enticing, though."

"Yeah, it was. Having a margarita at a brewery seems almost heretical, but I was sorely tempted."

"Another time, perhaps. I'll warn you—I don't make good decisions when tequila is involved. Just saying."

"Are you saying you want to make good decisions tonight?" The arched eyebrow challenged Olivia.

She took another sip of her beer to buy time. "When I wake up tomorrow, I don't want to wonder if my choices were made by me or tequila."

Keisha leaned back, sipping her beer with one hand while she pulled her phone out with the other. Olivia's heart sank at the blatant dismissal until she felt a touch on her ankle. Olivia shivered as

Keisha's ankle gently rubbed against her own. There was a ghost of a smile and a mischievous twinkle in Keisha's eyes as she nonchalantly scrolled through her phone. Olivia leaned back, mirroring her date as they played footsie under the table. They were both grinning by the time their food arrived.

Olivia eyed Keisha's burger enviously. "Damn, your bacon bleu burger looks amazing."

"Uh-huh."

"My vegan tacos look good, but I should have gotten the burger."

"Want a bite?"

"Are you sure? You know, germs and all?"

"Olivia, we've eaten each other's pussies. I'm pretty sure I'll be okay if you take a bite of my burger."

The damp spot forming in her undies during footsie became fully wet. "*Fuck.* Why did you have to mention pussy?"

"Here, have a taste." Keisha extended her burger across the table for Olivia to take a bite. "Good girl," Keisha purred.

Olivia moaned. She wasn't sure if the moan was because of the explosion of salty and savory in her mouth or because of the electric tingle running up her spine at being called a good girl. *Definitely both.*

"Now what were we talking about? That's right... *pussy.*" Keisha spoke the word with a sibilant drawl, supercharging Olivia's saturated core and popping goosebumps along her skin. "Last I heard, you were seemingly straight?"

She took a full swig of her IPA to irrigate her desiccated throat. "I've had the opportunity to re-evaluate some things in light of new data."

Her date laughed, full and throaty. "Hmm. Go on."

"While there is no firm conclusion, the preliminary analysis indicates the earlier assumption of strict heterosexuality was the result of incomplete information."

"Was it now," Keisha crooned. "I wonder if you need another data sample."

"More experience would help."

"Well, I can't possibly assist in your data collection efforts on an empty stomach. Now be a *good girl* and eat your vegan *tacos*." Keisha's emphasis on the word, "taco" contained an infinite amount of lewd potential.

"Mm hm," Olivia mewled, unable to trust herself to speak. She ground her thighs together in a desperate gambit to prevent the back of her dress from becoming a sodden mess. Biting into her taco provided a welcome distraction from the euphoria singing in her veins from being called a "good girl" once again, although each bite of her meal was now associated with the mental image of Keisha's thighs spread wide.

Chapter 24

All Fired Up

Pat Benatar

Keisha hid a smile behind her burger. *Olivia seemed to get a thrill from being called a "good girl." Dominance and submission don't really push any of my buttons, but if Olivia is a bit subby, then I'm happy to play into those tendencies. I'm glad she didn't catch my close call earlier. I almost said the wrong 'L' word. At least I caught myself and used "like" instead. Why would I even come close to saying "love" right now? It must be this whirlwind of emotions I'm experiencing regarding her. I need to watch what I say from now on. Letting the 'L' word slip would be disastrous.* Composing herself, she concentrated on her burger and the night ahead.

They finished their meals, opting to skip dessert. Keisha made a trip to the restroom while Olivia arranged transportation. She checked herself in the mirror, straightening her dress and giving her lip gloss a quick touch up. Her heart beat faster, thumping against her rib cage, as she rejoined Olivia. They waited far enough away from the doorway to avoid the cold air creeping in whenever it opened.

Damn, green looks good on her. Mmm, and a lifetime of hockey has definitely blessed Olivia with an exceptional ass. Not just a great butt, either. I should tell her to wear her hair up more often. Her neck would make a vampire weep for joy. I know I'd like to run my tongue up and down it all night long.

Keisha shook her head, but standing next to Olivia was like being a bee in a field full of wildflowers. Ankles, hips, fingers, and shoulders made intermittent contact, each small collision sending shockwaves through her nervous system. Each touch made her crave another.

Their ride arrived, and they ventured out into the frigid night, huddling together as they raced for the waiting vehicle. Scrambling into the backseat, they came to an unspoken mutual agreement to sit next to each other, snuggling for warmth and the electrifying thrill of the other's body pressed up against their own.

"These shoes look amazing but are not built for this weather," Keisha complained into Olivia's hair.

"True, but you are so fucking sexy." The blonde giggled, "I'd even call you a *knockout*."

Keisha groaned. "I'd be mad at your jokes, except you look too cute." She breathed in, inhaling Olivia's heady musk of vanilla, aloe, and sweat. Her body relaxed into her date.

Olivia molded herself into Keisha, sighing contentedly. "Is this okay?"

She folded an arm around the other woman. "We're good."

Arriving at Olivia's, they made another mad dash from the car to the building, shivering as Olivia fumbled to gain entry. Gorgon greeted them by flopping down and rolling around. Keisha admired her date's ass as she squatted down to greet the friendly feline. Unable to resist the allure of soft fur, she dropped onto her haunches to join the lovefest.

As their fingers intermingled in Gorgon's silky coat, Olivia raised her head enough to catch Keisha's eye. "It's cold, wet, and gross outside." Her pale skin flushed along her cheekbones as she continued, "You could stay here tonight...if you want."

"I don't know," Keisha drawled as she fought the urge to grin.

"My heater sucks, but I have lots of blankets, and we'll be warm if we snuggle."

She couldn't stop the mini-quake which emanated from her overheated core and sent a shiver through her body. Nor could she contain the accompanying heart flutter when she replied, "I've heard the most efficient method of sharing body heat requires no clothes."

Olivia dropped to her knees as her legs gave out. Recovering, she responded, "My heater sucks a *lot*, so we'll need to be extremely efficient."

Keisha tapped a fingertip to her chin, pretending to ponder the offer before replying in a husky tone, "I'd feel bad if I left you here to freeze with only Gorgon for company."

Matching grins spread across their faces as they stood.

"I have one of those spare toothbrushes from the dentist, if you want."

Keisha chuckled. "Are you hinting at something?"

The poor woman turned beet red. "No. I mean—"

"I'm teasing you. Thank you for the offer. Why don't we get ready for bed?"

"Mmm hmm."

They removed their shoes and unzipped each other, carefully hanging up the dresses. Olivia hadn't been joking about the heater because goosebumps were popping up all over. Keisha brushed her teeth side-by-side with Olivia before they dashed to the bed. Safely ensconced under the blankets, they melted into a full body kiss. Keisha ran her hands up Olivia's muscular flank, feeling the pebbly texture of her goosebumps. At the same time, Olivia's knee was nudging for an opening. Relaxing, she basked in the smooth feeling of a long, powerful leg sliding between her own. There was a whimpering noise when Olivia's thigh fully wedged itself between her legs. It took Keisha a moment to realize the whimper came from her throat.

Probing hands explored flexing muscles across strong backs and skin subtly slicking with sweat. Pebbled nipples rubbed against firm mounds as tongues feinted and jousted. Short fingernails danced lightly up Keisha's back, then down, slipping furtively under her waistband to caress and knead her quivering glutes. She moaned into Olivia's mouth before sending her hands on a similar exploratory mission. Keisha took a double handful of Olivia's perfectly perky posterior, drawing forth an answering groan. She raised her wrists, causing Olivia's waistband to slide down her ass.

"Wait. Wait. Please stop."

Keisha leaned back, extricating her hands. "Too much?"

"Yes. Maybe."

"Do you need to talk about it?" The last thing Keisha wanted to do was talk. Her engine was howling like an F-14 ready for take-off.

"I just feel like we're moving so fast. We already fucked before, and the aftermath wasn't pleasant. Maybe we could take it slower." She hesitated, voice dropping. "Just for tonight, if you're okay."

"You're such a *good girl* for telling me this—" Olivia's answering shiver confirmed the power of her words. Keisha wanted to fuck, and she wanted to fuck *now*. Her tongue traced the outline of her lips as she studied her bedmate. *I could fuck her now and make her beg for it. She so desperately wants to please me. To be my* good girl. *Part of me wants to be the manipulative bitch who bends her to my will, but I've already traveled down a similarly dark path with Olivia, and I wasn't comfortable. I want...I* need *to let my hate go and embrace whatever this is. Which means I need to back off and let things play out at her pace.*"—so why don't we slow down and keep our panties on?"

"Actually, my panties are soaking wet. They need to come off so my cunt doesn't catch a cold."

Keisha chuckled, planting a chaste kiss on Olivia's lips. "I'm in the same, mostly submerged, boat. Underwear off?"

"Yes, but let's just keep our fingers and mouths to themselves."

"Oh." Her mouth turned down involuntarily.

"No, wait. I mean keep our fingers and mouths away from each other's pussies. I still want to touch you and kiss you."

"Mmm. Perfect," Keisha purred as she wiggled off her drenched drawers.

Olivia's fingertips gently traced the blooming rose recently tattooed over Keisha's left breast. "Your tattoos are beautiful."

"How come you don't have any?"

She sighed. "My parents. Maxim. My own hang-ups. Take your pick."

"What would you get if you got one?"

"I'm not sure. I don't know what would look good on me."

"Baby, *anything* would look good on you. You live in the Rose City and play on the Blossoms. Lots of options with roses or hockey skates."

"Does it hurt?"

Keisha chortled. "Depending on your pain tolerance and where you get the ink, it can hurt *a lot,* but it's a survivable pain. And the end result is worth it. Plus, I'll be there to hold your hand if you want."

"Roses. I'd like roses," Olivia murmured.

"Are you falling asleep?"

The answer came in the form of a shy nod and a snuggle.

"Do you want me to spoon you?"

"Yes, please," she whispered before giving Keisha a kiss. Olivia rolled over, and Keisha melted into her. They lay joined together for several minutes before Olivia mumbled, "I love you."

Keisha felt a shock race from her brain to her toes and back. Before she could say anything, she heard a soft snore.

Chapter 25

C'Mon Let's Go

Girlschool

O livia felt warm as she drifted out of sleep. No, she felt hot. Sometime in the night, Gorgon must have crawled under the blankets because she was pressed against Olivia's chest. The small cat chirped and oozed out from her cozy blanket cave, pausing long enough to give Olivia an eyeful of brown star before she hopped down onto the floor. More pertinent to Olivia's superheated state was Keisha draped across her back. Their legs were tangled up, and Keisha's right hand was firmly attached to Olivia's left boob. Her bedmate was snoring directly into her ear, a sound she found endlessly annoying when Maxim did it, but surprisingly comforting from Keisha.

As pleasant as her wake-up was, she needed to extricate herself before the gathering dew between her legs received unwelcome company. With patience and deliberate movements, she made her escape to the bathroom before disaster struck. She contemplated putting on underwear, but decided to forgo it in case morning sex was on the menu.

I might not have been feeling emotionally ready for sex last night, but I am hotwired and ready to ride now. She stood up when she was done, washed her hands, then brushed her teeth. She opened the door to find Keisha staring at her from the bed. *Something's wrong. I can tell.*

"Good morning," she said with as much cheer as she could muster.

Keisha grunted and swung herself out of bed, sliding past Olivia into the bathroom.

Olivia took this opportunity to quickly feed Gorgon. Her teeth were chattering by the time she finished. She dove back into the warm bed as Keisha opened the bathroom door.

"Hi. Come join me."

Keisha's head swiveled back and forth, looking between her clothing from yesterday and Olivia. With her lips set in a firm line, Keisha stepped toward the discarded clothes.

"Please. Keisha," she begged. "Please talk to me."

The other woman halted, sluggishly wheeling on her back heel. Keisha crawled into the bed, pulling blankets and arms around herself defensively. She kept her eyes studiously locked on her knees, avoiding all contact.

Olivia kept her hands to herself, even as her heart begged for the chance to touch Keisha. "I'm sensing something is wrong, and I'm confused. Did I fart on you in the night?"

The corner of Keisha's mouth twitched upward, but her eyes remained focused elsewhere. "You don't remember?"

Beads of sweat popped on Olivia's brow. Her chest hitched as she struggled to breathe, body trembling as she swayed. "Remember what? What did I do?" The edges of her vision grew gray and dim.

Keisha's voice was a bare whisper. "As you fell asleep, you said, 'I love you.'"

"Oh. Shit."

"What does 'oh, shit' mean?"

"I was tired, and it must have slipped out."

Olivia couldn't read Keisha's expression. She could see shock and disbelief, but she couldn't determine if the other woman was angry or not. She definitely didn't seem pleased.

"Slipped out. Again, what do you mean?"

She balled her fists in the blankets and took a deep breath. Leaning forward, Olivia felt the heat in her face and voice. "Because I'm fucking falling in love with you, Keisha Owens, and I'm absolutely fucking terrified about what comes next."

"How can you be in love with me? We were barely speaking before yesterday."

Olivia screeched in frustration. "I didn't fall in love with you *yesterday*. I've been falling for you bit by bit for a while. It's the little things. How you talk to teammates, getting Cat's guy tickets and a jersey, and all these tiny things you do without even thinking about it. I didn't *allow myself to hope,* so I buried my feelings, or thought I did. Maybe I didn't want to say 'I love you' out loud because I know you'll reject me." She buried her face in her hands.

In a barely audible whisper, Keisha responded, "What if I don't reject you?"

Her head rose from the cradle of her palms, vision blurred from salt water welling in the corners of her eyes. "You don't?"

"No, I don't." Keisha's words were accompanied by a forceful exhalation, as if her lungs expelled half a lifetime's worth of tension. "I'm not going to say those words. I'm just not there."

Olivia was overburdened with words. Far too many to express adequately, so instead she vaulted forward, pressing her lips to Keisha's. Her initial reaction was hard and frigid, but a raging inferno of passion swiftly thawed the ice into a raging torrent. Strong fingers fisted a hank of Olivia's hair and yanked her further into Keisha's mouth. Their tongues clashed like the sticks of two centers at the faceoff circle, battling for dominance.

The strong hand hauled her away. "Since we're being honest, remember when I told you our sex was below average?"

She nodded, still feeling the sting of shame.

"I lied. It was fantastic, and I haven't stopped thinking about what your mouth did to me. I wondered how good you could be with practice." Keisha pulled the blankets down, exposing her naked form. "Would you like to eat me again?"

Olivia whimpered, "Yes, please."

"*You're such a good girl,*" Keisha purred. Olivia's sex was instantly saturated. She grabbed Keisha's legs and hauled her into a comfortable position, diving on her bared petals. She lavished her lover's labia with long, languid strokes, remembering the instructions to use her neck and shoulders to reduce strain on her tongue and give Keisha the tonguelashing of a lifetime. Using her left elbow to rest on, Olivia's left fingers teased Keisha's pussy in tandem with her tongue. Meanwhile, her right hand found a home between her own legs, feverishly fucking herself.

A hand tapped her head. "Mmm Mmm. Good girls don't multitask. A good girl would focus all of her attention on the feast before her. Don't worry, I'll take care of your pretty little kitty soon enough."

Olivia redoubled her efforts, teasing and suckling Keisha's clit while her fingers caressed the textured roof of Keisha's pussy, overloading the G-spot. She rode along as Keisha's hips rolled and bucked. Fingers slid into her hair, holding her in place as her lover grunted and moaned. Each lap of her tongue tickled her tastebuds with Keisha's musky and sweaty flavor.

I would happily dine at this buffet every night.

Keisha's fingers grew more insistent, pressing Olivia's face into her pussy, gyrating her hips. No longer able to effectively use her neck, Olivia's tongue began to fatigue, but she persevered. Keisha began coming apart, cries reverberating on the concrete walls. After a series of wild, erratic hip thrusts which threatened to break Olivia's nose, Keisha relaxed with a guttural groan.

"Mmm, you've been a good girl. You deserve a treat." She smiled wearily. "But first, I need you to kiss me." Olivia gleefully obliged. Keisha's hands roamed across her breasts, back, and butt as their lips playfully parted. Their tongues no longer battled for dominance, now content to cohabitate the same space. Keisha brought her hand down on one ass cheek with a clangorous crack. The sharp pain and booming sound summoned an involuntary moan and whimper from Olivia. "You *liked* being spanked, didn't you?"

Olivia mewled, "Yes." She felt a surge of embarrassment. She'd never reacted positively to being spanked before. "I'm sorry. It's weird."

"No, baby. It's not."

"You're not the first person to ever spank me, but somehow, it...wow," Olivia said shyly.

"Mmm, we'll explore your newfound kink later. Meanwhile, as much as I love tasting myself on your lips, it's my turn." Olivia let herself be pushed onto her back as Keisha slithered down, taking time for stops at her nipples and abdomen. Those brown eyes stayed locked on her own, promising extravagant delight. Keisha delivered.

The first gentle swipe on her clit sent shockwaves and shivers throughout her body. She heard a purr down below, as a firm tongue tip tantalized her engorged love button. A whimper escaped her throat as the circling stopped. Another whimper soon followed as Keisha moved down, slurping up her lower lips. She felt the tip open her up, braving her watery depths.

"Damn, girl. You are *wet*. Are you this turned on for me?'

"*Yes,*" she hissed. "I need you."

"I've been thinking about our night together—" Gentle kisses graced her inner thighs. "Have you?"

"Yes. I think about it every night. I dream about *you*, and what you do to me." More kisses, this time closer to the apex. "Please, Keisha." She was begging again, and she didn't care.

"As you wish." Brown eyes glittered with mischief as Keisha's glorious tongue once more irrigated Olivia's furrow. Fingers soon joined the tongue. Squelching and slurping filled her ears as Keisha supped on her slit.

Olivia's fingers crept down to the thick, wiry curls atop Keisha's head. There was a brief glower, but no protest. Two fingers were joined by a third. Teeth nibbled gently in between languid ovals on her clit.

Her breath grew short and her hands fell to her sides, frantically gripping the sheets. Keishs's free hand reached out to intertwine fingers as Olivia held on for dear life. The sensations emanating from her core overrode any instructions from her beleaguered brain.

Hips bucked wildly and lungs burned oxygen as Olivia struggled to contain the building eruption. Whatever was coming promised heaven, provided she lived long enough. Suddenly, there was just enough extra pressure on both sides of her clitoris. Olivia exploded as a triumphant cry ripped from her tattered throat as her body arched. The electricity ultimately subsided, and she collapsed back onto the mattress.

"I love you, Keisha. You don't have to say it back. I'm not saying this because my brain is broken, even though it is. I mean it. I love you. Thank you for not rejecting me."

Keisha crawled up Olivia's body while she babbled. Her lover planted a kiss to effectively shut up any words or thoughts. They made out in rapturous repose, melting slowly into each other. Sometime later, the pace of their kisses increased, and hands accelerated from gentle caresses to full-out fondles.

"Before we go for round two, I want to thank you for the best orgasm of my life. It was a knockout by Knockout."

"You're welcome, Olivia." Keisha flashed a happy smile. "Liv. I like Liv."

"I like it, too," Liv purred, observing her pale fingers toying with Keisha's coffee-colored chest. She pinched a pebbled nipple, bending down to take the other in her mouth. Once she'd tormented Keisha enough, she withdrew. "I have something special for you. Your reward for my best orgasm ever."

"Hmm?"

"Just wait." Olivia rolled out of bed and padded across the cold floor to her small closet. She reached up to the top shelf to grab a box.

"Nice view," she heard from behind her.

She pulled down her toy box, extracting the items she wanted. Olivia strutted back to the bed, lube in one hand and curved steel in the other. Keisha stared dubiously at the C-shaped metal bar with different sized bulbs at each end. "What have you got for me?"

"My favorite dildo."

Keisha's expression was dubious. "How does it work?"

Olivia's mouth curled toward her ears. "You'll see. Trust me." Applying lubricant to one end, she put the bottle down and crawled over to her lover. "I'm going to warm it up for you, then it's all yours." The cold steel touched her moist entrance, causing her to shiver. The sensation passed as she worked it inside of her, the metal quickly warming up. She groaned as the heavy steel stimulated her G-spot. Once the dildo was warm enough, she pulled it out.

"Spread your legs, my love."

Keisha complied, expression more curious now after witnessing Olivia's reaction. Olivia pressed the steel ball at Keisha's entrance, then worked it slowly inside, kissing her all the while. Once inserted, she began rubbing it on the roof of Knockout's pussy. She knew from personal experience how the heavy steel felt and was rewarded by a gleeful groan.

Her lover moaned and mewled against her lips, soon lost in the motion of the curved wand. It took only a few minutes before Keisha was coming apart once more. Olivia slowed down as she recovered before ramping up again. Keisha came again. Then another time. Soon, she was panting and begging Olivia for more. Twisting and churning her arm, Olivia brought Keisha to a plateau where one orgasm merged with the next, and then the next.

No longer able to kiss Keisha because the other woman's head tossed continuously in a tempest of ecstasy, Olivia instead descended on her small, pert breasts. She flicked and sucked while manipulating the wand, driving Keisha to new peaks.

"Stop... You... Have... To... *Fuck*... I can't... No more..."

Olivia placed the steel wand to the side and molded her body to her gasping lover's.

"Shh. I've got you, baby." And she did. She held Keisha as she drifted off to sleep, following soon after.

She woke up later to the insistent buzzing of her phone. Prying herself away from Keisha, she looked and saw Cathy's name on the screen.

"Yeah, Cat?"

"Liv," Cathy's urgent voice spilled from the speaker. "Practice is about to start. Where are you?"

"Oh, fuck me."

"Yeah, coach is pissed. I can't reach Keisha, either."

Keisha muttered groggily, "Huh? Who's calling?"

"*Holy shit,*" Cathy exclaimed.

"Cat..."

"*Holy shit, holy shit.* Are you with Keisha right now? Why does she sound drunk?"

"It's not—" *Yes, it's exactly what it sounds like, but I can't really tell Cathy about our morning of sex.* "We're not drinking." *Not helping yourself, Olivia.* Panicking, she blurted out, "Be there soon, bye," and hung up.

"Knockout, we gotta go. We're late for practice."

Keisha sat upright, although a subtle sway indicated she was still groggy. "We need to go." She sniffed. "We need to shower. I smell like sex," Keisha slurred. Another sniff against Olivia's neck. "You smell like sex, too."

"You're right, I'll get the shower started. We can shower together to save time."

"I'm not sure..." Keisha staggered to her feet. "I think I'm fuck drunk."

"You are. Look, no funny stuff in the shower. I'll be all business, I promise."

"Okay."

They mostly kept their promise, although helping each other wash inevitably led to extra touching and petting, which led to recriminations and giggles. Toweling off, they threw on clothes and summoned a ride while Olivia fed Gorgon. Arriving almost thirty minutes late, they geared up in the empty locker room and tottered toward the ice.

Hicks blew her whistle to summon the Blossoms. "Look here, everyone. Guess who finally decided to grace us with their presence." They looked down at their hands, not wanting to meet their teammates' gazes. "Just because the two of you score goals in buckets doesn't mean you can show up for practice whenever you want. Perhaps one of you would like to explain? Kennedy? Owens?" They remained silent, neither sure how to explain their tardiness. "Perhaps we need to do team wind sprints. Oh fine...Miller, you look like you're about to burst. What is it?"

Olivia looked up to see Cathy shaking her head vigorously. The poor woman did appear as if she was about to explode, but faithfully kept their torrid secret instead. "Coach. It's my fault."

The coach cast a dubious glare at the pink-haired winger. "Yes, Miller, please explain in exquisite detail why you are at fault for both Kennedy and Owens arriving late together..." Olivia witnessed comprehension dawn on Hicks' face. "*Holy shit.* It's about fucking time." She wheeled to address the team. "Okay, no need for wind sprints. Everyone get back to practice." When no one moved, she added, "Now what?"

Svetlana spoke up. "Are the two of you good now?"

Olivia's head swiveled to see Keisha staring back with an unsure expression. She smiled and nodded at her lover.

"We're in a much better place," Keisha answered. "There's still a lot to work through between us, but we've made progress."

Dani snorted loudly. "Oh yeah. Progressing all night long."

Hicks blew her whistle. "All right. You all have had your fun. Now get back to practice before I change my mind about wind sprints."

The team broke up with mutters of, "Yes, Coach."

Heike and Dani skated up and slapped Keisha and Olivia on their backs. Heike said with a grin, "Honestly, we figured the two of you who either murder each other or fuck it out."

"We're glad you two chose door number two," Dani finished her partner's thought.

Olivia cackled with a lecherous smile. "We are, too."

"Kennedy, Owens, a word when you're finished gossiping," Hicks snapped. They skated over to her. "You two owe me twenty burpees—*each*—before tonight's game as penance."

Chapter 26

Listen To Your Heart

Roxette

Keisha closed the door to her apartment and surveyed the room. Nothing had changed since she left it thirty hours ago. Her apartment's consistency stood in vivid contrast to the unsettled state of her mind and heart. She tossed her bag onto the bed and stripped off her clothes before stepping into the shower. Once clean and wearing fresh clothes, she pulled her phone off the charger and dialed her mother.

"Hey, Babygirl," Tamika greeted her daughter. "To what do I owe the pleasure?"

"Hi, Mama. Can't I just call because I want to hear your voice?"

"Always. Are you looking forward to tonight's game? Toronto is tough."

"Yes, Mama. We can beat them, though."

"I know you can."

"How's work?"

"Work is fine, Babygirl. Now are you going to talk about what's bothering you, or are we going to keep dancing?"

"Why do you think something's bothering me?"

"I'm your mother, sweetheart. Trust me. I know."

"I slept with her again, Mama. She told me she loves me."

"Mmm hmm. How do *you* feel about the Puck Princess?"

"She's not the Puck Princess. I mean, she is…a bit. We've been in therapy together, and there's more to her than just her stupid nickname."

"You're still not telling me how you feel."

"I like her, Mama. I'm scared of just how much I do." Keisha shivered, even as her heart raced. She could almost feel Olivia's fingertips tracing her tattoos, lips on her neck, searing hot pussy enveloping her fingers, and smooth thighs gliding along hers. More than just Olivia's skin, Keisha could hear her final faint murmur last night echo in the depths of her psyche, "*I love you.*"

Tamika replied in a smooth and even tone, "I'm not surprised."

Keisha felt a twinge of shock. "You're not?"

"Sweetheart, I've watched you mature into a beautiful and kind woman. I couldn't be more proud of you, of what you've overcome, of what you've accomplished. I know your Daddy would be proud of you, too. I just wish he'd had the opportunity to meet you before he died."

"Me too."

"When you first told me about you and…Olivia. I was upset. Not with you. I can't help but think of how she hurt you. I've been thinking more since then. You've changed so much over the years to fully grow into who you are. I guess I wondered if she'd done the same. The two of you have been linked for so long, I'm not surprised there are feelings between you."

"Oh, I…"

"Plus, she'd be an idiot not to love you."

Keisha roared with laughter. "Mama, stop."

"I'm serious, Keisha. You are beautiful inside and out. You could have any woman you want, Babygirl. Are you sure you want Olivia Kennedy?"

"I don't know."

"Tsk. You don't know, or you know but don't want to admit it? Because you've had a lot of girlfriends over the years, but you've never been serious about any of them. Is Olivia another pleasant way to keep your bed warm at night, or is she different?"

"What if I can't tell the difference?"

"Listen to your heart, sweetheart. It will know."

"Thanks, Mama." Keisha didn't share her mother's confidence.

"Aw, my sweet girl. I know you don't believe me, but you have a kind and generous heart. It won't lead you astray."

"I hope you're right."

"Trust your mama. Now go and get your head on straight for tonight. I'm inviting the ladies from church over to watch your game."

Keisha excitedly blurted out, "Oh, Mama. I forgot to tell you, we might be going to Norway for the World Championship series."

"Mmm hmm. *We* might be going. Congratulations to you and *Olivia,* because I *know* you'll be going to the World Championship."

Keisha couldn't help but notice the words her mother chose to emphasize. Before she could respond, Tamika muttered, "The World Championship is an afterthought to Olivia Kennedy, and yet my daughter somehow isn't sure of what she desires."

"I can hear you, Mama."

"Oh, you can? Go get ready, my silly goose, and listen to your heart."

"I will. I love you, Mama."

"I love you, too, Babygirl."

They ended the call, leaving Keisha to stare at her four walls. *My heart is telling me Olivia is putting in the work to be a better person. Volunteering, getting to know her teammates, making friends...overall not being the Puck Princess bitch I once knew. Maybe it won't last, but I feel like she's genuine. Also, Olivia is trusting me with her secrets and her past. She's more than just a good time in bed, and maybe Mama is right.*

She grabbed her book to distract herself from thoughts of Olivia. Reading Lavender LaFleur's latest bestseller was a poor choice in retrospect as the romance proved to be hot and steamy.

Arriving at the arena in time for pre-game preparations, Keisha was startled out of her mental preparations by Cathy seizing her arm. "Come on, Keisha. There's someone you need to meet." Cat dragged her in the direction of two tall men and Olivia's instantly recognizable blonde hair.

A gesture from one of the men caused Olivia to spin around, her smile measurable in the billions of lumens. "Knockout, meet my brother Pat and his partner, Bruce."

Pat was slightly taller than his sister, muscular and handsome—if you liked blond men. Bruce stood just over six feet tall, and definitely dark and handsome. *Apparently, Olivia and Pat both have a type...Black and gay.*

"Pleased to meet you, Keisha," Pat exclaimed with a dazzling grin. Keisha was immune to his looks, but his charm was undeniable. "I've heard so much about you over the years, but only good things of late."

"Ignore my husband. He's a cad," Bruce intervened with a megawatt grin. "Wonderful to meet you."

"It's great to meet you as well. Pat's the only member of Olivia's family she seems to like."

Bruce chuckled. "The rest of their family is *awful.* Or so, I've heard. They've obviously never met me." He threw the back of his hand against his forehead dramatically, adding, "Oh the shame of forbidden love."

"I don't think they'll ever meet me, either." Keisha reflected on her statement. *Because I won't be around long enough, or because they're bigots who can't handle their daughter being in love with another woman?*

Olivia wrapped her arms around Keisha. "It's their loss, because you are amazing. For the record, so is Bruce."

"And this is why you're my favorite sister-in-law."

"I'm your *only* sister-in-law."

Bruce waved her protest away with a smile. "Details."

Keisha faced Pat. "If I want dirt on Liv, I guess you're the one to talk to."

He smirked in response. "Oh, I have *all* the dirt on Livvy. What would you like to know?"

"Not cool, Pat. I'm your sister."

"Yes, but unlike your last paramour, I *like* this one." He grinned at Keisha. "Sweetie, you are a *vast* improvement over her insufferable fuckwad of an ex-fiancé."

She snorted with a smile. "I'm glad I could clear such a low bar."

"I know you all have to get ready for the game, but Bruce and I would love to take you out to dinner afterward—only if you want to, of course."

"Sounds wonderful. Can I hug you?"

Pat beamed, "Sweetie, you never have to ask."

She gave Pat and Bruce big hugs before heading to the locker room. Olivia fell into place beside her, slipping her arm into Keisha's. Keisha nearly missed a step in surprise. *We're publicly displaying intimacy now? I guess Olivia's okay with it.* Keisha sighed. *I am, too.* Her skin suddenly felt warm, in a very contented way.

"Thank you for being cool with Pat and Bruce. They surprised me."

Keisha's head snapped toward Olivia. "You didn't know they were coming?"

"No. I mean...I might have texted Pat this morning after...you know. Making love with you. Are you mad?"

"Should I be?"

"I hope not. Pat is my best friend as well as my brother, and of course I wanted you to meet him, it's just..."

"You're worried we're not at the 'meet the family' stage."

"Yeah."

"I called Mama after practice. I needed to talk to someone."

"And?" Olivia asked in a quiet voice.

"I'm not ready to introduce you to her yet, but we had a productive conversation. She told me to listen to my heart, so we'll see what it says."

"I trust your heart, Keisha. It's a good one."

Keisha surprised herself when they reached the door to the locker room. She halted just outside and swung Olivia around into a kiss.

"Wow. What was that for?"

"Luck, Liv. And because you're special. Now let's go." She punctuated her words with a swift smack on Olivia's ass. "I hope Hicks forgets about the burpees."

Hicks remembered.

Looking across the neutral zone at Toronto during warm-ups, Keisha's heart rate gathered speed. Toronto was fighting for a top spot in the league while Portland was slowly climbing out of the cellar and into playoff contention. Tonight was a must-win game, and Keisha could feel the tension in her muscles.

Olivia was on fire from the first face-off, feeding Keisha and Cathy with one perfect pass after another, but Toronto's goalie was a wall.

The first period ended with Portland down one. In the locker room, Cat and Liv pulled Keisha onto their bench to talk and offer encouragement. Hicks gave the team a pep talk and shuffled some lines, but she kept Keisa's line intact.

Toronto scored early in the second period against their line, increasing the lead to two. Keisha could almost hear Hicks' teeth grinding as they sat on the bench. She fanned on a shot on their next shift, negating a good scoring opportunity. Back on the bench, Olivia leaned in and whispered, "Make your next shot, and I'll eat you like a taco buffet tonight."

Keisha couldn't contain the giggle burbling out of her throat.

Hicks growled, "Something funny, Owens?"

"No, coach."

Three minutes later, their line was back on the ice. Cat popped the puck out from the corner for Olivia to scoop up. She crashed the net, flicking a last second pass to Keisha, who saw a sliver of space through the screen of bodies in front of the goalie and whipped a perfect shot into the back of the net.

The crowd's response was deafening, but Olivia's saucy wink was all the reward Keisha needed. Two shifts later, Keisha floated into the slot where Liv fed her a no-look pass. Keisha's one-timer lit the lamp again, tying the score.

Early in the third period, Misty's line forced an offensive zone face-off. Liv won the face-off, seeking Keisha. Their eyes met, and Keisha glanced to her right. Olivia took the hint and passed to Cathy in the slot. Keisha blocked the goalie's vision, and Cat whipped a five hole shot in to take the lead. It was bedlam in the Coliseum.

Through the flashing lights, wailing sirens, and clamorous cheers, Keisha read Olivia's lips as she said, "I love you."

Three shifts later, Cathy passed to Keisha who shouldered a defender aside. She skated in hot on her left wing, tracked by the goalie and remaining defender. There was a shot, but the window was tight. On instinct, Keisha eschewed her chance at the goal, firing low where the goalie made an easy pad save. The puck caromed off the goalie's leg pad where Liv pounced on it, firing top shelf past the outstretched glove of the diving goalie.

Cathy played the crowd like a giant symphony, conducting a chant of "Kay Oh, Kay Oh," as they skated to the bench. As the game clock ticked down, Keisha found the pink-haired winger jetting into neutral ice for an easy empty net goal for Cathy.

With a five-two win in hand, the team waddled to their dressing room. Caine flagged Keisha and Olivia, directing them to a post-game press conference. Sitting next to each other, they fielded questions about Portland's playoff prospects and the club's revitalized play. A reporter queried Olivia about her no-look passing.

Her answer was simple. "I trust Keisha implicitly. She always knows the best place to be. It's on me to make sure I get the puck there."

"Ms. Kennedy, another question. Can you comment on Maxim Kovalev's recent engagement announcement?"

Olivia's mouth hung open, speechless as she searched for a response.

Keisha snarled, "No, but I'll comment." She leaned over and tenderly tugged Olivia's chin forward. Their lips met, initially chaste.

Chastity commutated into intense ardor as their lips mashed together. Drawing apart, chests heaving, Keisha once again addressed the shocked press. "My girlfriend and I wish Maxim's poor fiancée the best."

Chapter 27

By Your Side

Sade

"**G**irlfriend?"

"Was I presumptuous?"

"A little, but I liked it." Olivia giggled. "I can't believe you decided to define the relationship in a press conference. You're amazing."

"I just hate bullshit gotcha questions. They needed a taste of their own medicine."

Olivia's mood deflated. Shoulders slumped, she asked in a quiet voice, "Are you saying you didn't mean it?"

Keisha stopped and wheeled to face her. "No, I'm sorry—" She shook her head, tight curls dancing. "I was angry with the reporter, but I meant what I said." Olivia shivered as Keisha gripped her arms. There was fire in those brown eyes. "Olivia Kennedy, will you officially be my girlfriend? In public and in private, with sappy displays of affection, vomitously cute text chains, and rudely spilling our popcorn when we make out in movie theaters?"

"Yes. Absolutely yes. You really thought this through, didn't you?"

Her girlfriend's eyes scrunched up adorably as she shrugged. "Maybe a little."

"Oh, is this one of those sappy displays of affection?"

"I think so."

Olivia bounced on the balls of her feet. "I like it. We should do more."

"Like in front of your brother at dinner tonight?"

She clapped a hand to her mouth. "I'm so excited about being your girlfriend I forgot my own brother. I'm a terrible sister."

"Somehow, I'm sure he'll forgive you."

"Let's go – we need to get changed."

They hustled into the locker room to find their entire team waiting to greet them with cheers, jeers, and catcalls. Keisha and Olivia waited patiently for the hubbub to die down before holding hands and curtsying deeply. "Thank you, everyone," Keisha intoned. "We appreciate your best wishes."

Coach Hicks clapped her hands and bellowed, "You've had your fun, now get out of here and enjoy yourselves, but not too much. I expect to see you all back here tomorrow. We host New York on Monday." Once the team filed out, Hicks focused on Keisha and Olivia. "Good job tonight. Kennedy, I have no idea how you pull off those no-look passes, but keep it up. There's no way you two aren't on the National squad after tonight."

"Thanks, coach."

They waited until Hicks left to high five and hug. The hug added caresses and was heading for a kiss when Olivia stepped back. "I know I owe you two orgasms, but we need to meet Pat and Bruce."

"Do I get to charge interest?"

Olivia's mouth curled into a grin, and she bounced her eyebrows up and down. "Maybe. For now, I need you to stop flirting with me." They managed to get in and out of the showers without further incident and only mild ogling.

"Pat wants to know about dinner. It's a Saturday, so things could be crazy."

"Hmmm. There's an Iraqi place, DarSalam, across the river on Alder. It's a quick ride on the MAX or bus. The food is great."

"Can we get a table?"

"Probably. Parking sucks around there. I suspect it'll be busy, but I like our chances."

"Give me the info so I can text Pat."

They met Pat and Bruce at the MAX station for a quick ride across the river. Keisha's prediction was correct, and they did get a table as the restaurant was mostly full. Olivia couldn't keep her eyes off Keisha as they discussed what to order. She looked beautiful in her Blossoms hoodie and yoga pants, chatting with Pat and Bruce as if they were old friends rather than strangers she'd just met.

Her reverie was broken when a young girl walked up to their table, mother in tow. The girl held out a bedazzled journal and a pen to Keisha. "Are you Keisha Owens? Would you sign my journal?"

"Of course, angel. What's your name?"

"Kim. I like watching you play."

"You do?" Keisha's voice rose slightly. "Do you want to play hockey when you grow up?"

"Maybe. I play roller derby. I'm a Rose Petal."

"Really now?" Olivia smiled as she beheld Keisha leaning in. "And where can I see you play roller derby?"

"Oaks Park. I'm just practicing now, but you can see me in September."

"I promise to come watch you. Maybe then I can get *your* autograph."

The girl whirled to face her mother. "Mommy, did you hear her? Keisha Owens is gonna want my autograph."

"Hey, Kim. I'd like you to meet my girlfriend, Olivia Kennedy. If you ask nicely, I bet she'll give you her autograph, too."

"Mommy, it's KO. This is so *cool*." The girl squealed delightedly as she stepped behind Keisha with her journal. Keisha twisted in her chair so she was knee-to-knee with Olivia. "Would you sign my journal?"

"Of course, Kim. Keisha and I will both be there to cheer for you. How old are you?"

"I'm almost eight," Kim said proudly.

"Keisha and I both started skating when we were young, too. I hope you love roller derby and stick with it, but if you don't, then find something else you love."

"Liv is right. Follow your heart"—Keisha pointed a finger at Kim's chest, then her forehead—"and your mind, and don't ever let anybody tell you 'no, you aren't allowed to do something, or you're not able.' Trust me, I've heard those words a lot in my life, but if your heart tells you it's right, then do it."

Kim clutched her signed journal to her chest. "Thank you. It was so nice meeting you. I'll see you later." Over Kim's shoulder, her mother added, "Thank you both. You're very kind." Olivia watched them walk away before spinning back to face her brother.

Pat exclaimed, "Oh my gosh, you two are so cute and amazing. Her face lit up when you said you would go watch her play."

"She's adorable. Speaking of..." Olivia and Keisha simultaneously pulled out their phones, typing feverishly. "Got it."

"Me too," Keisha echoed.

"You find her event schedule, and I'll look at our preliminary schedule for next season."

Keisha mused, "Hey, do you think we can sweet talk Caine and Hicks into a team field trip to watch junior roller derby? Maybe even throw in some swag?"

"I bet we can. Hmm. *Bet.* We can make a wager with Caine and Hicks. If the Blossoms make the playoffs, then they schedule a team field trip to watch these kids skate and bring a ton of merch to give out."

"Making the playoffs won't be easy."

"Knockout, the way you, me, and Cat are playing, we're going to win the Cup."

Keisha's answering grin was hungry. "Damn straight. Let's do this."

"Personally, I think you've got it in the bag," Pat added. "I haven't played hockey in forever, but you two and Miller have early '80s Oilers chemistry."

"You think so?"

"I do, Livvy. You're finally living up to your number. I couldn't be more proud of you. And you, Keisha. Your number sixty-four is perfect. The year the Civil Rights Act passed, I presume."

"You got it." Keisha nodded at the two men. "Any particular reason you decided to surprise Liv tonight?"

"*Well.* When I get a text from my little sister informing me she is madly in love, *of course* we booked a flight immediately."

Olivia's cheeks flushed as she shushed him. "I didn't say *madly,* Pat. And how did you get a flight on such short notice?"

"Madly was implied, my darling sister. How could you not be over the moon in love with this exquisite treasure before us? Mmm, watching Keisha skate tonight was almost enough to turn me straight. *Almost.* Ugh, and the flight was a nightmare. We had to route through Redmond and barely made the connection, but it was worth it."

"Exquisite treasure?" Keisha's grin was ear-to-ear.

Olivia's heart was racing as she observed the interplay between her brother and girlfriend. *For the first time in my life, everything just feels right. Well, almost everything. I still don't know if she loves me back.*

"He's not wrong. I'm just not as good with words as Pat is."

Pat laid a comforting hand on Keisha's arm. "Hopefully, other uses for her tongue make up for her lack of vocabulary."

Olivia hissed, "*Pat.*"

Keisha guffawed. "My lovely Liv promised to put her mouth where her money is tonight. She owes me *two* orgasms for my two goals."

"*Keisha.*" The rest of the table laughed as Olivia buried her beet red face in her hands. "I'm not speaking with you all for the rest of the night," she pouted. She felt Keisha's fingertips thread through her locks to massage her scalp.

"Oh, Liv. You know we love you."

Olivia's body stiffened. *Keisha's comment was so offhanded and casual.* She could hear snippets of conversation from other tables, but their table was deathly silent. Keisha's hand withdrew as Olivia's head pivoted at a glacial pace. She wanted to ask for clarification, but her throat refused to function. Her legs worked just fine, propelling her out of her seat and hurtling through the door, away from the unbearable silence.

On the sidewalk, she nearly ran over a strolling couple before fleeing down the street. Car horns honked as Olivia careened across the roadway. Tears clouded her vision, the sidewalk hazing in front of her. Strong arms grabbed her from behind as a horn trumpeted to the side.

Wiping tears from her eyes, Olivia belatedly saw the bus she almost ran in front of, the driver glaring daggers at her. Those strong arms lifted her out of the street and back onto the sidewalk while they spun her around to face Keisha.

"Liv, I'm sorry..."

"Sorry for what, Keisha? I understood when you said you weren't ready to say, 'I love you.' You're not there, and I'm okay with—"

Keisha cut her off with a sudden, hungry kiss. Olivia's arms flailed ineffectively at Keisha's back until her energy was spent. Hanging her arms limply around Keisha's waist, she leaned into the kiss, passion overtaking anger and humiliation.

After what seemed like an eternity, Keisha withdrew. "May I speak now?"

Olivia's head bobbed in assent.

Keisha inclined her head so their foreheads touched. She murmured, "When I told you I wasn't ready, I lied." Olivia's heart skipped a beat and her breath caught. "I lied to you. I lied to myself. The truth terrified me, so I buried it—deep. Mama told me to listen to my heart."

"What are you saying?"

"Let me get there, okay? A long time ago, I swore to myself I would get revenge for what you did to me. You hurt me when I was physically vulnerable, and now here you are, completely emotionally vulnerable. There's a part of me like a rut on a dirt road, just ingrained with the old desire to hurt you, but my heart is insisting I do something radical and beautiful instead."

Warm arms encircled Olivia's waist, and Keisha's forehead and nose pressed against her own. "I love you, Olivia Kennedy. I'm sorry the first time I said it so dismissively. Maybe I'm still trying to protect myself. I should have told you I love you earlier, I was—"

Olivia angled her chin forward, cutting off Keisha's words with her lips. She punctuated each word with a kiss. "Stop." *kiss* "Babbling." *kiss* "That's." *kiss* "My." *kiss* "Job."

She felt Keisha's fingertips brush away tears on her cheeks. "You're crying, baby."

"Happy tears, my love."

"Good. Now it's cold and we're hungry. May I escort you back to dinner?"

"Yes, but first, can you say it again?"

"I love you, Olivia Kennedy."

"I love you, too, Keisha Owens."

Acknowledgements

Thank you to my wife and partner, Cecily. I couldn't do this without you.

Lady Starlight, Merlin, and our dearly departed Francesca – you are a part of every cat in my books and a wonderful part of our lives.

Steve Davala, as always, thank you for encouraging me to try writing. Now I can't stop.

Thank you to the writing and reading community, in Portland and at-large. Community is what gets me through some days. I've met so many incredible people, in person and virtually. Life is better because of the community I've found along this journey.

Special thanks to Katherine and Grand Gesture Books. It's a truly welcoming space for romance lovers in Portland. Your support has meant a lot to me.

Also, thank you to Kim and all the wonderful people at Broadway Books. It's my neighborhood bookstore, and when I needed a location for one of my characters to meet her crush, it seemed only appropriate.

Finally, thank you to the Rose City Rollers community. Roller derby is my safe space.

About the author

Chris Walters is a romance author living in Portland, Oregon with his wife and two cats. When not reading, writing, or working his day job, he is an announcer for the Rose City Rollers. He self-published his first novel, No One Like You in 2024.